Jane Porter grew up on a diet of Mills & Boon® romances, reading late at night under the covers so her mother wouldn't see! She wrote her first book at age eight, and spent many of her high school and college years living abroad, immersing herself in other cultures and continuing to read voraciously. Now Jane splits her time between rugged Seattle, Washington, and the beautiful beaches of Hawaii, with her sexy surfer and three very active sons. Jane loves to hear from her readers. You can write to her at PO Box 524, Bellevue, WA 98009, USA. Or visit her website at www.janeporter.com

Recent titles by the same author:

HIS MAJESTY'S MISTAKE
  (A Royal Scandal)
NOT FIT FOR A KING?
  (A Royal Scandal)
A DARK SICILIAN SECRET
ONE CHRISTMAS NIGHT IN VENICE
  (Short Story)

For Randall Toye—
thank you for the friendship and support.

"Help me, Drakon," Morgan said, her voice pitched low, hoarse. "Do you *want* me to beg? Is that what you're asking me to do?"

Her chin lifted and tears sparkled in her eyes, even as her heart burned as if it had been torched with fire. "Am I to go onto my knees in front of you and plead my case?"

He didn't move a muscle. "I do like you on your knees," he said cordially.

She drew a ragged breath, locked her knees, praying for strength. "I haven't forgotten," she said, aware that she was in trouble here, aware that she ought to go. Now. "So on my knees it is," she said mockingly, lifting the hem of her pale blue skirt to kneel on his limestone floor.

Her mind was whirling, her insides churning. She felt sick, dizzy, off-balance by the contradictions and the intensity and her own desperation.

He had to help her.

He had to.

THE
FALLEN GREEK
BRIDE

BY
JANE PORTER

First published in Great Britain 2013
by Mills & Boon, an imprint of Harlequin (UK) Limited.
Harlequin (UK) Limited, Eton House, 18-24 Paradise Road,
Richmond, Surrey TW9 1SR

© Jane Porter 2013

ISBN: 978 0 263 23428 2

Harlequin (UK) policy is to use papers that are natural, renewable
and ͘ ͘ ͘ ͘ ͘ ͘ ble
fore
lega

Prin
by (

CHAPTER ONE

"Welcome home, my wife."

Morgan froze inside Villa Angelica's expansive marble and limestone living room with its spectacular floor-to-ceiling view of blue sky and sea, but saw none of the view, and only Drakon's face.

It had been five years since she'd last seen him. Five and a half years since their extravagant two-million-dollar wedding, for a marriage that had lasted just six months.

She'd dreaded this moment. Feared it. And yet Drakon sounded so relaxed and warm, so *normal,* as if he were welcoming her back from a little holiday instead of her walking out on him.

"Not your wife, Drakon," she said softly, huskily, because they both knew she hadn't been his anything for years. There had been nothing, no word, no contact, not after the flurry of legal missives that followed her filing for divorce.

He'd refused to grant her the divorce and she'd spent a fortune fighting him. But no attorney, no lawsuit, no amount of money could persuade him to let her go. Marriage vows, he'd said, were sacred and binding. She was his. And apparently the courts in Greece agreed with him. Or were bought by him. Probably the latter.

"You are most definitely still my wife, but that's not a conversation I want to have across a room this size. Do come in,

Morgan. Don't be a stranger. What would you like to drink? Champagne? A Bellini? Something a little stronger?"

But her feet didn't move. Her legs wouldn't carry her. Not when her heart was beating so fast. She was shocked by Drakon's appearance and wondered for a moment if it really was Drakon. Unnerved, she looked away, past his broad shoulders to the wall of window behind him, with that breathtaking blue sky and jagged cliffs and azure sea.

So blue and beautiful today. A perfect spring day on the Amalfi Coast.

"I don't want anything," she said, her gaze jerking back to him, although truthfully, a glass of cool water would taste like heaven right now. Her mouth was so dry, her pulse too quick. Her head was spinning, making her dizzy from nerves and anxiety. Who *was* this man before her?

The Drakon Xanthis she'd married had been honed, sleek and polished, a man of taut, gleaming lines and angles.

This tall intimidating man in front of the picture window was broader in the shoulders and chest than Drakon had ever been, and his thick, inky brown and black hair hung in loose curls to almost his shoulders, while his hard fierce features were hidden by a dark beard. The wild hair and beard should have obscured his sensual beauty, rendered him reckless, powerless. Instead the tangle of hair highlighted his bronzed brow, the long straight nose, the firm mouth, the piercing amber gold eyes.

His hair was still damp and his skin gleamed as if he'd just risen from the sea, the Greek god Poseidon come to life from ancient myth.

She didn't like it. Didn't like any of this. She'd prepared herself for one thing, but not this....

"You look pale," he said, his voice so deep it was almost a caress.

She steeled herself against it. Against him. "It was a long trip."

"Even more reason for you to come sit."

Her hands clenched into fists at her sides. She hated being here. Hated him for only seeing her here at Villa Angelica, the place where they'd honeymooned for a month following their spectacular wedding. It'd been the happiest month of her life. When the honeymoon was over, they had left the villa and flown to Greece, and nothing was ever the same between them again. "I'm fine here," she said.

"I won't hurt you," he replied softly.

Her nails pierced her skin. Her eyes stung. If her legs would function, she'd run. Protect herself. Save herself. If only she had someone else to go to, someone else who would help her, but there was no one. Just Drakon. Just the man who had destroyed her, making her question her own sanity. "You already did that."

"You say that, my love, and yet you've never told me how—"

"As you said, that isn't something to discuss across a room of this size. And we both know, I didn't come here to discuss us. Didn't come to rehash the past, bring up old ghosts, old pain. I came for your help. You know what I need. You know what's at stake. Will you do it? Will you help me?"

"Six million dollars is a lot of money."

"Not to you."

"Things have changed. Your father lost over four hundred million dollars of what I gave him."

"It wasn't his fault." She met his gaze and held it, knowing that if she didn't stand up to him now, he'd crush her. Just as he'd crushed her all those years ago.

Drakon, like her father, played by no rules but his own.

A Greek shipping tycoon, Drakon Sebastian Xanthis was a man obsessed with control and power. A man obsessed with amassing wealth and growing his empire. A man obsessed with a woman who wasn't his wife. Bronwyn. The stunning Australian who ran his Southeast Asia business.

Her eyes burned and her jaw ached.

But no. She wouldn't think of Bronwyn now. Wouldn't wonder if the willowy blonde still worked for him. It wasn't important. Morgan wasn't part of Drakon's life anymore. She didn't care whom Drakon employed or how he interacted with his female vice presidents or where they stayed on their business trips or what they discussed over their long dinners together.

"Is that what you really believe?" he asked now, voice almost silky. "That your father is blameless?"

"Absolutely. He was completely misled—"

"As you have been. Your father is one of the biggest players in one of the biggest Ponzi schemes ever. Twenty-five billion dollars is missing, and your father funneled five billion of that to Michael Amery, earning himself ten percent interest."

"He never saw that kind of money—"

"For God's sake, Morgan, you're talking to me, Drakon, your husband. I know your father. I know exactly who and what he is. Do not play me for a fool!"

Morgan ground her teeth together harder, holding back the words, the tears, the anger, the shame. Her father wasn't a monster. He didn't steal from his clients. He was just as deceived as they were and yet no one would give him an opportunity to explain, or defend himself. The media had tried and convicted him and everyone believed the press. Everyone believed the wild accusations. "He's innocent, Drakon. He had no idea Michael Amery was running a pyramid scheme. Had no idea all those numbers and profits were a lie."

"Then if he's so innocent, why did he flee the country? Why didn't he stay, like Amery's sons and cousins, and fight instead of setting sail to avoid prosecution?"

"He panicked. He was frightened—"

"Absolute rubbish. If that's the case, your father is a coward and deserves his fate."

She shook her head in silent protest, her gaze pinned to Drakon's features. He might not look like Drakon, but it was definitely him. She knew his deep, smooth voice. And those eyes. His eyes. She'd fallen in love with his eyes first. She'd met him at the annual Life ball in Vienna, and they hadn't danced—Drakon didn't dance—but he'd watched her all evening and at first she'd been discomfited by the intensity of his gaze, and then she'd come to like it. Want it. Crave it.

In those early weeks and months when he'd pursued her, Drakon had seduced her with his eyes, examining her, holding her, possessing her long before he'd laid a single finger on her. And, of course, by the time he did, she was his, completely.

The last five years had been brutal. Beyond brutal. And just when Morgan had found herself again, and felt hopeful and excited about her future, her world came crashing down with the revelation that her beloved, brilliant financier father, Daniel Copeland, was part of Michael Amery's horrific Ponzi scheme. And instead of her father handling the crisis with his usual aplomb, he'd cracked and run, creating an even bigger international scandal.

She drew a slow, unsteady breath. "I can't leave him in Somalia to die, Drakon. The pirates will kill him if they don't get the ransom money—"

"It would serve him right."

"He's my father!"

"You'll put yourself in debt for the rest of your life, just to buy his freedom, even though you know that his freedom will be short-lived?"

"Yes."

"You do understand that he'll be arrested the moment he tries to enter any North American or European country?"

"Yes."

"He's never going to be free again. He's going to spend

the rest of his life in prison, just like Michael Amery will, once he's caught, too."

"I understand. But far better for my father to be in an American prison than held by Somali pirates. At least in the United States he could get medical care if he's sick, or medicine for his blood pressure. At least he could have visitors and letters and contact with the outside world. God knows what his conditions are like in Somalia—"

"I'm sure they're not luxurious. But why should the American taxpayer have to support your father? Let him stay where he is. It's what he deserves."

"Do you say this to hurt me, or is it because he lost so much of your money?"

"I'm a businessman. I don't like to lose money. But I was only in four hundred million of the five billion he gave to Amery. What about those others? The majority were regular people. People who trusted your father with their retirement money…their life savings. And what did he do? He wiped them out. Left them with nothing. No retirement, no security, no way to pay the bills now that they're older and frailer and unemployable."

Morgan blinked hard to clear her vision. "Michael Amery was my father's best friend. He was like family. Dad trusted him implicitly." Her voice cracked and she struggled to regain her composure. "I grew up calling him Uncle Michael. I thought of him as my family."

"Yes, that's what you told me. Just before I gave your father four hundred million dollars to invest for me. I nearly gave him more. Your father wanted more. Twice as much, as a matter of fact."

"I am so sorry."

"I trusted your father." His gaze met hers and held. "Trusted you. I know better now."

She exhaled slowly. "Does that mean you won't help me?"

"It means…" His voice faded, and his gaze narrowed as

he looked at her, closely, carefully, studying her intently. "Probably not."

"Probably?" she repeated hoarsely, aware that if Drakon wouldn't help her, no one would. The world hated her father, and wanted him gone. They all hoped he was dead. And they all hoped he'd suffered before he died, too.

"Surely you must realize I'm no fan of your father's, *glykia mou*."

"You don't have to be a fan of my father's to loan me the money. We'll draft a contract, a legal document that is between you and me, and I will pay you back in regular installments. It will take time, but it'll happen. My business is growing, building. I've got hundreds of thousands of dollars of orders coming in. I promise—"

"Just like you promised to love me? Honor me? Be true to me for better or worse, in sickness and in health?"

She winced. He made it sound as if she hadn't ever cared for him, when nothing could be further from the truth. The truth was, she'd cared too much. She'd loved him without reservation. And by loving him so much, she'd lost herself entirely. "So why haven't you divorced me then? If you despise me so much, why not let me go? Set me free?"

"Because I'm not like you. I don't make commitments and run from them. I don't make promises and then break them. I promised five and a half years ago to be loyal to you, and I have been."

His deep gravelly voice was making her insides wobble while his focused gaze rested on her, examining her, as if she were a prized pet that had been lost and found.

"Those are just words, Drakon. They mean nothing to me. Not when your actions speak so much louder."

"My actions?"

"Yes, your actions. Or your lack of action. You only do something if it benefits you. You married me because it benefited you...or you thought it would. And then when times were difficult...when I became difficult...you disappeared. You wouldn't grant me a divorce but you certainly didn't come after me, fight for me. And then when the world turned against us, where were you again? Nowhere. God knows you wouldn't want your name sullied by connection with the Copeland family!"

He studied her for an endless moment. "Interesting how you put things together. But not entirely surprising. You've inherited your mother's flair for the dramatic—"

"I hate you! I do." Her voice shook and her eyes burned, but she wouldn't cry, wouldn't give him the satisfaction. He'd taken everything from her, but not anymore. "I knew you'd mock me, humiliate me. I knew when I flew here, you'd make it difficult, but I came anyway, determined to do whatever I had to do to help my father. You'll let me plead with you, you'll let me beg—"

"That was a very passionate speech, so please forgive my interruption, but I'd like to clarify something. I don't believe you've begged. You've asked for money. You've demanded money. You've explained why you needed money. But there's been very little pleading, and absolutely no begging, at all."

A pulse beat wildly in her throat. She could feel the same wild flutter in her wrists and behind her ears. Everything in her was racing, raging. "Is that what you want? You'd like for me to beg you to help me?"

His head cocked, and he studied her, his gaze penetrating. "It'd certainly be a little more conciliatory, and far less antagonistic."

"Conciliatory." She repeated the word, rolling it over in her mouth, finding it sharp and bitter.

He said nothing, just watched her, and she felt almost breathless at the scrutiny, remembering how it had been between them during their four weeks here on their honeymoon. It was in this villa she'd learned about love and lust, sex and pleasure, as well as pain and control, and the loss of control.

Drakon never lost control. But he'd made sure she did at least once a day, sometimes two or three times.

Their sex life had been hot. Explosive. Erotic. She'd been a virgin when she'd married him and their first time together had been uncomfortable. He was large and it had hurt when he entered her fully. He'd tried to make it pleasurable for her but she'd been so overwhelmed and emotional, as well as let down. She couldn't respond properly, couldn't climax, and she knew she was supposed to. Knew he wanted her to.

He'd showered with her afterward, and kissed her, and beneath the pulsing spray of the shower, he lavished attention on her breasts and nipples, the curve of her buttocks and the cleft between her thighs, lightly playing with her clit until he finally accomplished what he hadn't in bed—she came. One of his arms held her up since her legs were too weak to do the job, and then he'd kissed her deeply, possessively, and when she could catch her breath, he'd assured her that the next time he entered her, it wouldn't hurt. That sex would never hurt again.

It hadn't.

But that didn't mean sex was always easy or comfortable.

Drakon liked it hot. Intense. Sensual. Raw. Unpredictable.

He loved to stand across the room from her—just as he was doing now—and he'd tell her what to do. Tell her what he wanted. Sometimes he wanted her to strip and then walk naked to him. Sometimes he wanted her to strip to just her panties and crawl to him. Sometimes he wanted her to wear nothing but her elegant heels and bend over...or put a foot on a chair and he'd tell her where to touch herself.

Each time Morgan would protest, but he'd look at her from beneath his black lashes, his amber gaze lazy, his full mouth curved, and he'd tell her how beautiful she was and how much he enjoyed looking at her, that it gave him so much pleasure to see her, and to have her trust him....

Obey him...

She hated those words, hated the element of dominance, but it was part of the foreplay. They had good sex in bed, but then they had this other kind of sex—the sex where they played erotic games that pushed her out of her comfort zone. It had been confusing, but inevitably she did what he asked, and then somewhere along the way, he'd join her, and his mouth would be on her, between her legs, and his hands would hold her, fingers tight on her butt, or in her hair, or gripping her thighs, holding them apart, and he'd make love to her with his mouth and his fingers and his body and he'd arouse her so slowly that she feared she wouldn't ever come, and then just when the desire turned sharp and hurt, he'd relent. He'd flick the tip of his tongue across that small sensitive nub, or suck on her, or stroke her, or enter her and she'd break. Shatter. And the orgasms were so intense they seemed to go on forever. Maybe because he made sure they went on forever. And by the time he was finished, she was finished. There was nothing left. She was drained, spent, but also quiet. Compliant.

He loved her flushed and warm, quiet and compliant. Loved her physically that is, as long as she made no emotional demands. No conversation. No time, energy or patience. Required no attention.

Morgan's chest ached. Her heart hurt. She'd been so young then, so trusting and naive. She'd been determined to please him, her beautiful, sensual Greek husband.

Their honeymoon here, those thirty days of erotic lovemaking, had changed her forever. She couldn't even think of this villa without remembering how he'd made love to her in every single room, in every way imaginable. Taking her on chairs and beds, window seats and stairs. Pressing her naked back or breasts to priceless carpets, the marble floor, the cool emerald-green Italian tiles in the hall...

She wanted to throw up. He hadn't just taken her. He'd broken her.

"Help me out if you would, Drakon," she said, her voice pitched low, hoarse. "I'm not sure I understand you, and I don't know if it's cultural, personal or a language issue. But do you *want* me to beg? Is that what you're asking me to do?" Her chin lifted and tears sparkled in her eyes even as her heart burned as if it had been torched with fire. "Am I to go onto my knees in front of you, and plead my case? Is that what it would take to win your assistance?"

He didn't move a muscle and yet the vast living room suddenly felt very small. "I do like you on your knees," he said cordially, because they both knew that on her knees she could take him in her mouth, or he could touch her or take her from behind.

She drew a ragged breath, locked her knees, praying for strength. "I haven't forgotten," she said, aware that she was in trouble here, aware that she ought to go. Now. While she could. While she still had some self-respect left. "Although God knows, I've tried."

"Why would you want to forget it? We had an incredible sex life. It was amazing between us."

She could only look at him, intrigued by his memory of them, as well as appalled. Their sex life had been hot, but their marriage had been empty and shallow.

Obviously that didn't trouble him. It probably didn't even cross his mind that his bride had feelings. Emotions. Needs. Why should it? Drakon's desires were so much simpler. He just needed her available and willing, as if she were an American porn star in a rented Italian villa.

"So on my knees it is," she said mockingly, lifting the hem of her pale blue skirt to kneel on his limestone floor.

"Get up," he growled sharply.

"But this *is* what you want?"

"No. It's not what I want, not like this, not because you need something, want something. It's one thing if we're making love and there's pleasure involved, but there's no pleasure in seeing you beg, especially to me. The very suggestion disgusts me."

"And yet you seemed so charmed by the memory of me on my knees."

"Because that was different. That was sex. This is…" He shook his head, features tight, full mouth thinned. For a moment he just breathed, and the silence stretched.

Morgan welcomed the silence. She needed it. Her mind was whirling, her insides churning. She felt sick, dizzy and off balance by the contradictions and the intensity and her own desperation.

He had to help her.

He had to.

If he didn't, her father was forever lost to her.

"I've no desire to ever see my wife degrade herself," Drakon added quietly, "not even on behalf of her father. It actually sickens me to think you'd do that for him—"

"He's my father!"

"And he failed you! And it makes me physically ill that you'd beg for a man who refused to protect you and your sisters and your mother. A man is to provide for his family, not rob them blind."

"How nice it must be, Drakon Xanthis, to live, untouched and superior, in your ivory tower." Her voice deepened and her jaw ached and everything in her chest felt so raw and hot. "But I don't have the luxury of having an ivory tower. I don't have any luxuries anymore. Everything's gone in my family, Drakon. The money, the security, the houses, the cars, the name…our reputation. And I can lose the lifestyle, it's just a lifestyle. But I've lost far more than that. My family's shattered. Broken. We live in chaos—"

She broke off, dragged in a breath, feeling wild and unhinged. But losing control with Drakon wouldn't help her. It would hurt her. He didn't like strong emotions. He pulled away when voices got louder, stronger, preferring calm, rational, unemotional conversation.

And, of course, that's what she'd think about now. What Drakon wanted. How he liked things. How ironic that even after five years, she was still worrying about him, still turning herself inside out to please him, to be what *he* needed, to handle things the way *he* handled them.

What about her?

What about what she needed? What she wanted? What about her emotions or her comfort?

The back of her eyes burned and she jerked her chin higher. "Well, I'm sorry you don't like seeing me like this, but this is who I am. Desperate. And I'm willing to take desperate measures to help my family. You don't understand what it's like for us. My family is in pain. Everyone is hurting, heartsick with guilt and shame and confusion—how could my father do what he did? How could he not know Amery wasn't investing legitimately? How could he not protect his clients…his friends…his family? My sisters and brother—we can't even see each other anymore, Drakon. We don't speak to each other. We can't handle the shame of it all. We're outcasts now. Bottom feeders. Scum. So fine, stand there and mock me with your principles. I'm just trying to save what I can. Starting with my father's life."

"Your father isn't worth it. But you are. Stop worrying about him, Morgan, and save yourself."

"And how do I do that, Drakon? Have you any advice for me there?"

"Yes. Come home."

"Home?"

"Yes, home to me—"

"You're not home, Drakon. You were never home."

She saw him flinch and she didn't like it, but it was time he knew the truth. Time he heard the truth. "You asked me a little bit ago why I'd want to forget our sex life, and I'll tell you. I don't like remembering. It hurts remembering."

"Why? It was good. No, it was great. We were unbelievable together—"

"Yes, yes, the sex was hot. And erotic. You were an incredibly skillful lover. You could make me come over and over, several times a day. But that's all you gave me. Your name, a million-dollar diamond wedding ring and orgasms. Lots and lots of orgasms. But there was no relationship, no communication, no connection. I didn't marry you to just have sex. I married you to have a life, a home. Happiness. But after six months of being married to you, all I felt was empty, isolated and deeply unhappy."

She held his gaze, glad she'd at last said what she'd wanted to say all those years ago, and yet fully aware that these revelations changed nothing. They were just the final nail in a coffin that had been needing to be sealed shut. "I was so unhappy I could barely function, and yet there you were, touching me, kissing me, making me come. I'd cry after I came. I'd cry because it hurt me so much that you could love my body and not love me."

"I loved you."

"You didn't."

"You can accuse me of being a bad husband, of being cold, of being insensitive, but don't tell me how I felt, because I know how I felt. And I did love you. Maybe I didn't say it often—"

"Or ever."

"But I thought you knew."

"Clearly, I didn't."

He stared at her from across the room, his features so hard they looked chiseled from stone. "Why didn't you tell me?" he said finally.

"Because you hated me talking to you." Her throat ached and she swallowed around the lump with difficulty. "Every

time I opened my mouth to say anything you'd roll your eyes
or sigh or turn away—"

"Not true, either."

"It is true. For me, it's true. And maybe you were raised in
a culture where women are happy to be seen and not heard,
but I'm an American. I come from a big family. I have three
sisters and a brother and am used to conversation and laughter and activity and the only activity I got from you was sex,
and even then it wasn't mutual. You were the boss, you were
in control, dictating to me how it'd be. Strip, crawl, come—"
She broke off, gasping for air, and shoved a trembling hand
across her eyes, wiping them dry before any tears could fall.
"So don't act so shocked that I'd beg you to help me save my
father. Don't say it's degrading and beneath me. I know what
degrading is. I know what degrading does. And I've been
there, in our marriage, with you."

And then she was done, gone.

Morgan raced to the door, her heels clicking on the polished marble, her purse on the antique console in the grand
hall close to the front door, her travel bag in the trunk of her
hired car.

She'd flown to Naples this morning from London, and
yesterday to London from Los Angeles, almost twenty hours
of traveling just to get here, never mind the tortuous wind-
ing drive to the villa perched high on the cliffs of the coast
between Positano and Ravello. She was exhausted and flattened. Finished. But she wasn't broken. Wasn't shattered, not
the way she'd been leaving him the first time.

Count it as a victory, she told herself, wrenching open the
front door and stepping outside into the blinding sunshine.
*You came, you saw him and you're leaving in one piece. You
did it. You faced your dragon and you survived him.*

CHAPTER TWO

DRAKON WATCHED MORGAN spin and race from the living room, her cheeks pale, her long dark hair swinging. He could hear her high-heeled sandals clicking against the gleaming floor as she ran, and then heard the front door open and slam shut behind her.

He slowly exhaled and focused on the silence, letting the stillness and quiet wash over him, calm him.

In a moment he'd go after her, but first he needed to gather his thoughts, check his emotions. It wouldn't do to follow her in a fury—and he was furious. Beyond furious.

So he'd wait. He'd wait until his famous control was firmly in check. He prided himself on his control. Prided himself for not taking out his frustrations on others.

He could afford to give Morgan a few minutes, too. It's not as if she would be able to go anywhere. Her hired car and driver were gone, paid off, dispensed with, and the villa was set off the main road, private and remote. There would be no taxis nearby. She wasn't the sort to stomp away on foot.

And so Drakon used the quiet and the silence to reflect on everything she'd said. She'd said quite a bit. Much of it uncomfortable, and some of it downright shocking, as well as infuriating.

She'd felt degraded in their marriage?

Absolute rubbish. And the fact that she'd dare say such

a thing to his face after all these years made him want to throttle her, which seriously worried him.

He wasn't a violent man. He didn't lose his temper. Didn't even recognize the marriage she described. He had loved her, and he'd spoiled her. Pampered her. Worshipped her body. How was that degrading?

And how dare she accuse him of being a bad husband? He'd given her everything, had done everything for her, determined to make her happy. Her feelings had been important to him. He'd been a respectful husband, a kind husband, having far too many memories of an unhappy childhood, a childhood filled with tense, angry people—namely his mother—to want his wife to be anything but satisfied and content.

His mother, Maria, wasn't a bad woman, she was a good woman, a godly woman, and she tried to be fair, just, but that hadn't made her affectionate. Or gentle.

Widowed at thirty-five when Drakon's father died of a heart attack at sea, Maria had found raising five children on her own overwhelming. The Xanthis family was wealthy and she didn't have to worry about money, but that didn't seem to give her much relief, not when she was so angry that Drakon's father, Sebastian, had died leaving her with all these children, children she wasn't sure she'd ever wanted. One child might have been fine, but five was four too many.

Drakon, being the second eldest, and the oldest son, tried to be philosophical about her anger and resentment. She came from a wealthy family herself and had grown up comfortable. He told himself that her lack of affection and attention wasn't personal, but rather a result of grief, and too many pregnancies too close together. And so he learned by watching her, that she was most comfortable around her children if they asked for nothing, revealed no emotion or expressed no need. Drakon internalized the lesson well, and by thirteen and fourteen, he became the perfect son, by having no needs, or emotions.

But that didn't mean he didn't enjoy pleasing others. Throughout his twenties he had taken tremendous pride in spoiling his girlfriends, beautiful glamorous women who enjoyed being pampered and showered with pretty gifts and extravagant nights out. The women in his life quickly came to understand that he didn't show emotion and they didn't expect him to. It wasn't that he didn't feel, but it wasn't easy to feel. There were emotions in him somewhere, just not accessible. His girlfriends enjoyed his lifestyle, and his ability to please them, and they accepted him for who he was, and that he expressed himself best through action—doing or buying something for someone.

So he bought gifts and whisked his love interests to romantic getaways. And he became a skilled lover, a patient and gifted lover who understood the importance of foreplay.

Women needed to be turned on mentally before they were turned on physically. The brain was their largest erogenous zone, with their skin coming in second. And so Drakon loved to seduce his partner slowly, teasing her, playing with her, whetting the appetite and creating anticipation, because sex was how he bonded. It's how he felt close to his woman. It was how he felt safe expressing himself.

And yet she hadn't felt safe with him. She hadn't even enjoyed being with him. Their lovemaking had disgusted her. He had disgusted her. He'd turned off Morgan.

Drakon's stomach heaved. He swallowed the bitter taste in his mouth.

How stupid he'd been. Moronic.

No wonder she'd left him. No wonder she'd waited until he had flown to London for the day. He had only been away for the day, having flown out early on his jet, returning for a late dinner. But when he had entered their villa in Ekali, a northern suburb of Athens, the villa had been dark. No staff. No dinner. No welcome. No Morgan.

He remembered being blindsided that night. Remembered

thinking, he could go without dinner, could live without food, but he couldn't live without Morgan.

He'd called her that night, but she didn't answer. He'd left a message. Left another. Had flown to see her. She wasn't to be found.

He'd called again, left another message, asking her to come home. She didn't. She wouldn't even speak to him, forcing him instead to interact with her trio of attorneys as they informed him that their client was filing for divorce and moving on with her life, without him.

His surprise gave way to frustration and fury, but he never lost his temper with her. He tried to remain cool, focused, pragmatic. Things had a way of working out. He needed to be patient, and he refused to divorce her, insisting he wouldn't agree to a divorce until she met with him. Sat down and talked with him. In person.

She wouldn't. And so for two years her attorneys had battled on her behalf, while Drakon had battled back. His wife would not leave him without giving him a proper explanation. His wife could not just walk away on a whim.

While the Copeland attorneys filed their lawsuits and counter lawsuits, Drakon had made repeated attempts to see Morgan. But every attempt to reach her was stymied. Her cell phone was disconnected. He had no idea where she was living. Her family would only say she'd gone away indefinitely. Drakon had hired private investigators to find her, but they couldn't. Morgan had vanished.

For two and a half years she'd vanished into thin air.

And then in October she had reappeared, emerging again on the New York social scene.

The private investigators sent Drakon her address, a high-rent loft in SoHo, paid for by her father. She'd started her own business as a jewelry designer and had opened a small shop down the street from her loft, locating her little store close to big hitters.

Drakon immediately flew to New York to see her, going straight from the airport to her boutique, hoping that's where he'd find her at 11:00 a.m. on a Wednesday morning. Before he even stepped from his limousine, she walked out the shop's front door with her youngest sister, Jemma. At first glance they looked like any glamorous girls about town, slim and chic, with long gleaming hair and their skin lightly golden from expensive spray-on tans, but after that first impression of beauty and glamour, he saw how extremely thin Morgan was, dangerously thin. She looked like a skeleton in her silk tunic and low-waisted trousers. Wide gold bangles covered her forearms, and Drakon wondered if it was an attempt to hide her extreme slenderness, or perhaps accent her physique?

He didn't know, wasn't sure he wanted to know. The only thing he knew for certain was that she didn't look well and he was baffled by the change in her.

He let her go, leaving her with Jemma, and had his driver take him to her father's building on 53rd and Third Avenue. Daniel Copeland could barely hide his shock at seeing Drakon Xanthis in his office, but welcomed him cordially—he was, after all, taking care of Drakon's investment—and asked him to have a seat.

"I saw Morgan today," Drakon had said bluntly, choosing not to sit. "What's wrong with her? She doesn't look well."

"She hasn't been well," Daniel answered just as bluntly.

"So what's wrong with her?" he repeated.

"That's her business."

"She's my wife."

"Only because you won't let her go."

"I don't believe in divorce."

"She's not happy with you, Drakon. You need to let her go."

"Then she needs to come tell me that herself." He'd left Daniel's office after that, and for several weeks he'd expected a call from Morgan, expected an email, something to say she was ready to meet with him.

But she didn't contact him. And he didn't reach out to her. And the impasse had continued until three days ago when Morgan had called him, and requested a meeting. She'd told him up front why she wanted to see him. She made it clear that this had nothing to do with them, or their marriage, but her need for a loan, adding that she was only coming to him because no one else would help her.

You are my last resort, she'd said. *If you don't help me, no one will.*

He'd agreed to see her, telling her to meet him here, at Villa Angelica. He'd thought perhaps by meeting here, where they'd embarked on their married life, they could come to an understanding and heal the breach. Perhaps face-to-face here, where they had been happy, he could persuade Morgan to return to Athens. It was time. He wanted children, a family. He wanted his wife back where she was supposed to be—in his home, at his side.

Now he realized there was no hope, there never had been, and he felt stupid and angry.

Worse, he felt betrayed. Betrayed by the woman he'd vowed to love and protect, a woman he'd continued to love these past five years, because it was his duty to love her. To be faithful to her. To provide for her.

But he was done with his duty. Done with his loyalty. Done with her.

He wanted her gone.

It was time to give her what she wanted. Time to give them both what they needed—freedom.

Drakon ran a hand over his jaw, feeling the dense beard, a beard he'd started growing that day he'd learned she intended to end their marriage without uttering a single word, or explanation, or apology to him.

He'd vowed he'd grow his beard until his wife returned home, or until he'd understood what had happened between them.

It had been an emotional, impulsive vow, but he'd kept it. Just as he'd kept hope that one day Morgan, his wife, would return to him.

And she had returned, but only to tell him how much she hated him. How much she despised him. How degrading she'd found their marriage.

Drakon exhaled slowly, trying to control the hot rush of emotion that made his chest ache and burn. He wasn't used to feeling such strong emotions. But he was feeling them now.

He headed into the small sitting room, which opened off the living room to his laptop and his briefcase. He took a checkbook to his personal account out of his briefcase and quickly scrawled her name on a check and filled in the amount, before dating it and signing it. He studied the check for a moment, the anger bubbling up, threatening to consume him, and it took all of his control to push it back down, suppressing it with ruthless intent.

He wasn't a failure. She was the failure. She was the one who had walked out on him, not the other way around. He was the one who had fought to save their marriage, who had honored their vows, who had honored her by thinking of no other woman but his wife, wanting no other woman than Morgan.

But now he was done with Morgan. He'd give her the money she wanted and let her go and once she left, he wouldn't waste another moment of his life thinking or worrying about her. She wanted her freedom? Well, she was about to get it.

Morgan was standing on the villa's front steps gazing out at the sweeping drive, with the stunning view of the dark green mountains that dropped steeply and dramatically into the sapphire sea, anxiously rubbing her nails back and forth against her linen skirt, when she heard the front door open behind her.

Her skin prickled and the fine hair at her nape lifted. She knew without even turning around it was Drakon. She could feel his warmth, that magnetic energy of his that drew everything toward him, including her.

But she wouldn't allow herself to be drawn back into his life. Wouldn't give him power over her ever again.

She quickly moved down the front steps, putting distance between them. She refused to look at him, was unable to look at him when she was filled with so much anger and loathing.

"You had no right to send away my car," she said coolly, her gaze resolutely fixed on the dazzling blue and green colors of the coast, but unable to appreciate them, or the lushness of the dark pink bougainvillea blooming profusely along the stone wall bordering the private drive. Panic flooded her limbs. He was so close to her she could barely breathe, much less think.

"I didn't think you'd need it," he said.

She looked sharply at him then, surprised by his audacity, his arrogance. "Did you imagine I was going to stay?"

"I'd hoped," he answered simply.

She sucked in a breath, hating him anew. He could be so charming when he wanted to be. So endearing and real. And then he could take it all away again, just like that. "You really thought I'd take one look at you and forget my unhappiness? Forget why I wanted the divorce?"

"I thought you'd at least sit down and talk to me. Have a real conversation with me."

"You don't like conversation, Drakon. You only want information in bullet form. Brief, concise and to the point."

He was silent a moment, and then he nodded once, a short, decisive nod. "Then I'll be brief in return. The helicopter is on the way for you. Should be here soon. And I have this for you." He handed her a folded piece of paper.

Morgan took it from him, opened it. It was a check for seven million dollars. She looked up at Drakon in surprise. "What's this?"

"The money you begged for."

She flinched. "The pirates are only asking for six."

"There will be other expenses. Travel and rescue logistics. You'll want to hire an expert to help you. Someone with the right negotiation skills. There are several excellent firms out there, like Dunamas Maritime Intelligence—"

"I'm familiar with them."

"They won't be cheap."

"I'm familiar with their fees."

"Don't try to do it on your own, thinking you can. Better to pay for their expertise and their relationships. They know what they're doing, and they'll help you avoid a trap. The Somali pirates sound like they're a ragtag organization, but in truth, they're being funded by some of the wealthiest, most powerful people in the world."

She nodded, because she couldn't speak, not with her throat swelling closed. For the first time in a long, long time, she was grateful for Drakon Xanthis, grateful he had not just the means to help her, but knowledge and power. There weren't many people like Drakon in the world, and she was suddenly so very glad he had been part of her life.

"Use whatever is left after you pay your management fee to pay your father's travel expenses home. There should be enough. If there isn't, let me know immediately," he added.

"Thank you," she whispered huskily.

His jaw tightened. "Go to London before you return to New York, cash the check at the London branch of my bank. There won't be any problems. They'll give you the six million in cash you need for the ransom. You must have it in cash, and not new bills, remember that. But I'm sure your contact told you that?"

"Yes."

His lashes dropped, concealing his expression. "They're very particular, *agapi mou.* Follow the instructions exactly. If you don't, things could turn unpleasant."

"As if storming my father's yacht off the Horn of Africa, and killing his captain, wasn't unpleasant enough—" She broke off, hearing the distinctive hum of the helicopter. It was still a distance from them, but it would be here soon.

For a moment neither said anything, both listening to the whir of the helicopter blades.

"Why have you kept the news of your father's kidnapping private?" he asked her. "I would have thought this was something you'd share with the world...using the kidnapping to garner sympathy."

"Because it wouldn't garner sympathy. The American public hates him. Loathes him. And if they discovered he was kidnapped by Somali pirates, they'd be glad. They'd be dancing in the streets, celebrating, posting all kinds of horrible comments all over the internet, hoping he'll starve, or be killed, saying it's karma—"

"Isn't it?"

She acted as though Drakon hadn't spoken. "But he's my father, not theirs, and I'm not using their money. Not spending government funds, public funds or trust funds. We haven't gone to the police or the FBI, haven't asked for help from anyone. We're keeping this in the family, handling it on our own, and since my brother and sisters don't have the means, I'm using my money—"

"You mean my money."

She flushed, and bit hard into her lower lip, embarrassed. His money. Right. They weren't married, not really, and she had no right to spend his money, just because she had nothing left of her own.

"I stand corrected," she whispered. "Your money. I'm using your money. But I will pay you back. Every penny. Even if it takes me the rest of my life."

A small muscle popped in his jaw. "There is no need for that—" He paused, glancing up at the dark speck overhead. The helicopter.

One of the reasons Drakon had chosen this villa for their honeymoon five and a half years ago was that the outdoor pool had a special cover that converted it into a heli landing pad, making the remote villa far more appealing for a man who needed to come and go for meetings in Naples, Athens and London.

"No need to pay me back," Drakon said, picking up his broken train of thought, "because I'm calling my attorney this afternoon and asking him to process the paperwork for the divorce. He will make sure the dissolution is expedited. By the end of the month, it will be over."

It will be over. For a moment Morgan couldn't take this last bit in. What was he saying? He'd finally agreed to the divorce?

He was giving her the money *and* granting her the divorce?

She just looked up at him, eyes burning, too overwhelmed to speak.

He dipped his head and raised his voice in order to be heard over the hum of the helicopter, which had begun to descend. "You will receive your full settlement once the dissolution occurs. With the current state of affairs, I'd suggest you allow me to open a personal account for you in London or Geneva and I can deposit the funds directly into the account without fear of your government freezing it. I know they've frozen all your family accounts in the United States—"

"I don't want your money."

"Yes, you do. You came here for my money. So take what you came for—"

"I came to see you for my father, and that was the only reason I came here today."

"A point you made abundantly clear." He smiled at her

but his amber gaze looked icy, the golden depths tinged with frost. "So I am giving you what you wanted, freedom and financial security, which fulfills my obligation to you."

She shivered at the hardness in his voice. She had never heard him speak to her with so much coldness and disdain and it crushed her to think they were ending it like this—with contempt and anger.

"I'm sorry," she whispered, her heart beating too fast and aching far too much.

He didn't answer her, his gaze fixed on the helicopter slowly descending. Morgan watched him and not the helicopter, aware that this just might be the last time she would see Drakon and was drinking him in, trying to memorize every detail, trying to remember him. This.

"Thank you," she added, wanting him to just look at her, acknowledge her, without this new terrible coldness.

But he didn't. He wouldn't. "I'll walk you to the landing pad," he said, putting his hand out to gesture the way without touching her or looking at her.

Perhaps it was better this way, she told herself, forcing herself to move. It was hard enough being near him without wanting to be closer to him. Perhaps if he'd been kind or gentle, she'd just want more of him, because she'd always wanted more of him, never less. The doctors had said she was addicted to him, and her addiction wasn't healthy. He wasn't the sun, they lectured her, and Drakon, despite his intense charisma and chemistry, couldn't warm her, nor could he actually give her strength. She was the only one who could give herself strength, and the only way she could do that was by leaving him, putting him behind her.

And so here she was again, leaving him. Putting him behind her.

So be strong, she told herself. *Prove that you're strong on your own.*

Morgan blinked to clear her vision, fighting panic as they

rounded the villa and walked across the lawn for the open pool terrace where the helicopter waited, balancing like a peculiar moth on the high-tech titanium cover concealing the pool. The roar from the helicopter's spinning blades made conversation impossible, not that Drakon wanted to talk to her.

One of the household staff met them at the helicopter with Morgan's travel bag and Drakon set it inside the helicopter, then spoke briefly to the pilot before putting out his hand to assist Morgan inside.

She glanced down at his outstretched hand, and then up into his face, into those unique amber eyes that had captivated her from the start. "Thank you again, Drakon, and I hope you'll be happy."

His lips curved, but his eyes glittered with silent fury. "Is that a joke? Am I supposed to be amused?"

She drew back, stunned by his flash of temper. For a moment she could only stare at him, surprised, bewildered, by this fierce man. This was a different Drakon than the man she'd married. This was a Drakon of intense emotions and yet after they'd married she'd become convinced that Drakon felt no emotion. "I'm serious. I want you to be happy. You deserve to be happy——"

"As you said I'm not one for meaningless conversation, so I'm going to walk away now to save us from an embarrassing and uncomfortable goodbye," he said brusquely, cutting her short, to propel her into the helicopter. Once he had her inside, he leaned in, his features harsh, and shouted to her, "Don't try to cut corners, Morgan, and save money by handling the pirates yourself. Get help. Call Dunamas, or Blue Sea, or one of the other maritime intelligence companies. Understand me?"

His fierce gaze held hers, and she nodded jerkily, even as her stomach rose up, and her heart fell. If he only knew...

If he only knew what she had done....

And for a split second she nearly blurted the truth, how she had been negotiating with the pirates on her own, and how she'd thought she was in control, until it had all gone terribly wrong, which was why she was here...which was why she needed Drakon so much. But before she could say any of it, Drakon had turned around and was walking away from the helicopter.

Walking away from her.

Her eyes burned and her throat sealed closed as the pilot handed Morgan a set of headphones, but she couldn't focus on the pilot's instructions, not when she was watching Drakon stride toward the villa.

He was walking quickly, passing the rose-covered balustrade on the lower terrace then climbing the staircase to the upper terrace, and the entire time she prayed he'd turn around, pray he'd acknowledge her, pray he'd wave or smile, or just *look* at her.

He didn't.

He crossed the terrace to the old ballroom and disappeared into the great stone house without a backward glance.

So that was it. Done. Over. She was finally free to move on, find happiness, find love elsewhere.

She should be happy. She should feel at peace. But as the helicopter lifted off the pad, straight into the air, Morgan didn't feel any relief, just panic. Because she didn't get the help she needed, and she'd lost him completely.

It wasn't supposed to have gone like this. The meeting today...as well as their marriage. Because she had loved him. She'd loved him with everything she was, everything she had, and it hadn't been enough. It should have been enough. Why wasn't it enough? In the beginning she'd thought he was perfect. In the beginning she'd thought she'd found her soul mate. But she was wrong.

Seconds passed, becoming one minute and then another as the helicopter rose higher and higher, straight up so that the villa fell away and the world was all blue and green, with the sea on one side and the sharp, steep mountains on the other and the villa with its famous garden clinging to that bit of space on the rock.

Fighting tears, her gaze fell on the check she still clutched in her hand. Seven million dollars. Just like that.

And she'd known that he'd help her if she went to him. She'd known he'd come through for her, too, because he'd never refused her anything. Drakon might not have given her much of his time or patience, but he'd never withheld anything material from her.

Guilt pummeled her, guilt and fear and anxiety, because she hadn't accomplished everything she'd come to Villa Angelica to accomplish. She needed more from Drakon than just a check. She needed not just financial assistance, but his help, too. There were few men in the world who had his knowledge of piracy and its impact on the shipping industry. Indeed, Drakon was considered one of the world's leading experts in counter piracy, and he'd know the safest, quickest method for securing her father's release, as well as the right people to help her.

Morgan exhaled in a rush, heart beating too hard.

She had to go back. Had to face Drakon again. Had to convince him to help her. Not that he'd want to help her now, not after everything that was said.

But this wasn't about pride or her ego. This was life and death, her father's life, specifically, and she couldn't turn her back on him.

Swallowing her fear and misgivings, Morgan grabbed at her seat belt as if throwing on brakes. "Stop, wait," she said to the pilot through the small microphone attached to her headphones. "We have to go back. I've forgotten something."

The pilot was too well-trained, and too well-paid, to question her. For a moment nothing seemed to happen and then he shifted and the helicopter began to slowly descend.

* * *

Drakon didn't wait for the helicopter to leave. There was no point. She was gone, and he was glad. While climbing the stairs to his bedroom suite, he heard the helicopter lift, the throbbing of the rotary blades vibrating all the way through the old stone walls.

In his bathroom, Drakon stripped his clothes off and showered, and then dried off, wrapping the towel around his hips and prepared to shave. It would take a while. There was a lot of beard.

He gathered his small scissors and his razor and shaving cream, and as he laid everything out, he tried not to think, particularly not of Morgan, but that was impossible. He was so upset. So angry.

What a piece of work she was. To think he'd wanted her back. To think he'd loved her. But how could he have loved her? She was shallow and superficial and so incredibly self-centered. It was always about her...what she wanted, what she needed, with no regard for anyone else's needs.

As he changed the blade on his razor, he felt a heaviness inside, a dull ache in his chest, as if he'd cut his heart. And then Drakon took the razor to his beard.

He had loved her, and he had wanted her back. Wanted her home with him. But that was before he understood how disgusted she was with him, how disgusted she'd been by their marriage.

Disgust.

He knew that word, and knew disgust produced shame. His mother used to be disgusted by emotion, and as a young child, Drakon had felt constant shame in her presence, shame that he had such strong emotions, emotions she found appalling. He still remembered how wild he'd felt on the inside as a little boy, how desperate and confused he'd felt by her rejection, and how determined he'd been to win her affection, even if it meant destroying part of himself. And so that became the goal, his sole objective as a child. To master his hideous emotions. To master want and need, to stifle them, suppress them, thereby winning his mother's approval and love.

He succeeded.

Drakon rinsed the shaving cream from his face and studied his smooth, clean jaw in the mirror. He'd forgotten what his face looked like without a beard, had forgotten how lean his cheeks were above his jutting chin. He had a hard chin, a stubborn chin, which was fitting since he knew he'd become a very hard, stubborn man.

A knock sounded on the outer door of his suite. Drakon mopped his damp face, grabbed a robe and crossed his room to open the door, expecting one of the villa staff.

It wasn't one of the staff. It was Morgan.

Something surged in his chest, hot and fierce, and then it was gone, replaced by coldness. Why was she back? What game was she playing now? He leaned against the door frame, and looked her up and down, coolly, unkindly. "Need more money already?"

Color stained her cheeks, making her blue eyes even deeper, brighter. "You...shaved."

"I did."

"We need to talk."

He arched an eyebrow. "Thank you, but no. I've heard more than enough from you already. Now if you'd be so good as to see yourself out, and get back into the helicopter—"

"The helicopter is gone. I sent him away."

"That was foolish of you. How are you getting back home?"

"We'll figure that out later."

"You mean, you can figure that out later. There is no more we. I'm done with you, and done helping you. You've got your check, and in a month's time you'll receive your settlement, but that's it. That's all there is. I've nothing more for you. Now if you'll excuse me, I have things to do."

Her eyebrows lifted and she walked past him, into his room, glancing around the impressive bedroom where they'd spent the first month of their marriage. "Looks just as I remembered," she said, turning to face him. "But you don't. You've changed."

"Yes, I grew a beard, I know."

"It's not just the beard and hair. It's you. You're different."

"Perhaps you weren't aware. My wife left me. It wasn't an easy thing."

She gave him a long, level look. "You could have come after me."

"I did."

"You did not."

"I *did.*"

"I'm not talking about phone calls, or emails or texts. Those don't count."

"No, they don't, and they don't work, either, not once you turned your phone off. Which is why I flew repeatedly to New York, drove up to Greenwich—"

"You didn't!"

His hands clenched at his sides. "Good God, if you contradict me one more time, I will throttle you, Morgan, I will. Because I did go after you, I wanted you back, I wanted you home and I did everything I could to save our marriage. I visited your father at work. I appeared on your parents' doorstep. I spoke—repeatedly—to each of your siblings—"

"I can't believe it," she whispered.

"Believe it," he said grimly, moving toward her, stepping so close he could smell the hint of fragrance from her shampoo, and the sweet clean scent of her perfume on her skin. He loved her smell. Loved her softness. Loved everything about his woman.

But that was then, and this was now, and he was so done with the craziness and the chaos that had followed their marriage.

His gaze caught hers, held, and he stared down into her eyes, drinking in that intense blue that always made him think of the sea around his home in Greece. Tiny purple and gold flecks shimmered against the deep blue irises...like the glimmer of sun on the surface of water. He used to think her eyes perfectly expressed who she was...a woman of magic and mystery and natural beauty.

Now he knew he'd been tricked. Tricked and deceived by a beautiful face, by stunning blue eyes.

Bitterness rolled through him and his gut clenched, his jaw hardening, anger roiling. He really didn't like remembering, and he really didn't like feeling the fury and rejection again, but it was what it was. They were what they were. Such was life.

"And if you don't believe me, make some enquiries. Ask your brother, or your sister Tori, or Logan, or Jemma. Ask them all. Ask why no one would tell me anything. Demand answers, if not for you, then for me. Find out why the entire Copeland family turned their backs on me. I still don't know why. Just as I don't know why you disappeared, or where you went, but you were gone. I even hired private investigators, but you were nowhere to be found."

Morgan bundled her arms across her chest and drew a slow, unsteady breath. A small pulse beat wildly at the base of her throat. "You really came after me?"

"Of course I came after you! You were my wife. You think I just let you go? You think I'd just let you leave?"

She swallowed hard, her blue eyes shining. "Yes."

He swore softly, and walked away from her, putting distance between them. "I don't know what kind of man you think you married, but I am not he. In fact, you, my wife, know nothing about me!"

She followed him, her footsteps echoing on the tiled floor. "Maybe that's because you never gave me a chance to get to know you, Drakon."

He turned abruptly to face her, and she nearly bumped into him. "Or maybe it's because you didn't stay long enough to get to know me, *Morgan.*"

Morgan took a swift step backward, stunned by his blistering wrath. She squeezed her hands into fists, crumpling the check in her right hand.

The check.

She'd forgotten all about it. Her heart ached as she glanced down at the paper, creased and crumpled in her hand. "If that is truly the case," she said, voice husky, "I'm sorry."

"If," he echoed bitterly, his upper lip lifting. "I find it so ironic that you don't believe a word I say, and yet when you need something, you'll come running to me—"

"I didn't want to come to you."

"Oh, I'm quite sure of that." He made a rough sound and turned away, running a hand over his newly shaven jaw. "My God, what a joke. I can't believe I waited five years for this."

"What does that mean?"

"Forget it. I don't want to do this." He turned and looked at her, cheekbones jutting against his bronzed skin, his amber gaze hard. "I have finally come to the same realization you did five years ago. That we don't work. That we never worked. That there is no future. And since there is no future, I've nothing to say to you. You have the money, you have what you came for—"

"I didn't just come for money. I need your help."

"That's too bad, then, because the check is all you're getting from me."

She inhaled sharply. He sounded so angry, so bitter, so unlike her husband. "Drakon, please. You know how the pirates operate. You've dealt with them before—"

"No. Sorry. I'm not trying to be ugly, just honest. I'm done. Done with you. Done with your family. Done with your father—my God, there's a piece of work—but he's not my problem anymore, because I'm not his son-in-law anymore, either. And I never thought I'd say this, but I'm actually glad to be done…glad to have a complete break. You've exhausted every one of my resources, and I've nothing more to give. To you, or the rest of the Copeland family."

She winced and looked away, hoping he didn't see the tears that filled her eyes. "No one told me you came after me," she said faintly, her gaze fixed on the view of the sea beyond the window. "But then, in that first year after I left you, no one told me anything."

"I don't see how that is relevant now."

"It probably won't mean anything to you now, but it's relevant to me. It's a revelation, and a comfort—"

"A *comfort?*" he repeated sarcastically.

She lifted her chin a fraction, squared her shoulders. "Yes, a comfort, knowing you didn't give up on me quickly, or easily."

"Unlike you, who gave up so quickly and easily."

"I'm sorry."

"I'm sure you are, now that the privileged Copelands are broke."

She laughed to keep from crying. He was so very, very changed. "We're broke," she agreed, "every last one of us, and struggling, but my brother and sisters, they're smart. They'll be fine. They'll come out of this okay. Me…I'm in trouble. I'm stupid—"

"If this is a play for my sympathy, it's not working."

"No. I'm just telling you the truth. I'm stupid. Very, very stupid. You see, I didn't come to you first. I tried to handle the pirates on my own. And I've already given them money—"

"What?"

She licked her lower lip. "We didn't want it known about my father, and so we kept the details to ourselves, and I tried to manage freeing my father on my own, and I gave them money. But they didn't free my father."

Drakon just looked at her, his jaw clenched, his lips a hard flat line. She could see the pulse beating at the base of his throat. His amber gaze burned. He was furious.

Furious.

Morgan exhaled slowly, trying to calm herself, trying to steady her nerves, but it wasn't easy when her heart raced and the blood roared in her ears. "I didn't want to have to bother you, Drakon. I thought I could manage things better than I did."

He just kept staring at her, his spine stiff, his muscles tensed. He was clearly at war within himself and Morgan felt his anger and frustration. He wanted to kick her out of the villa but he didn't run from responsibilities, or from providing for his family.

He was Greek. Family was everything to him. Even if he didn't enjoy his family.

His tone was icy cold as he spoke. "You should have never tried to handle the pirates on your own. You should have gone to Dunamas or Blue Sea immediately—"

"I didn't have the money to pay for outside help or expertise," she said softly, cutting him short, unable to endure another lecture. "I didn't even have enough to pay the three million ransom. You see, that's what they asked for in the beginning. Three million. But I couldn't come up with exactly three million, and I'd run out of time, so I made the sea drop with what I had, thinking that almost three million was better than nothing, but I was wrong. The pirates were really angry, and accused me of playing games, and they were now doubling the ransom to six million and I had just two weeks or they'd execute Dad."

"How much were you short?"

"A hundred thousand."

"But you dropped two-point-nine million?"

She nodded. "I was so close to three million, and to get it I emptied my savings, sold my loft, liquidated everything I had, but I couldn't get more. I tried taking out personal loans from family and friends but no one was able to come up with a hundred thousand cash in the amount of time we had."

"You didn't come to me for the hundred thousand."

"I didn't want to involve you."

"You have now."

"Because there was no one else who would help me. No other way to come up with six million without my father's situation becoming public knowledge."

"One hundred thousand would have been a hell of a lot cheaper than six million."

"I know." Her stomach heaved. She felt so terribly queasy. "But then, I told you I was stupid. I was afraid to come to you, afraid to face you—"

"I wouldn't have hurt you."

"No, but I have my pride. And then there were all those feelings—" she broke off, and gulped air, thinking she might just throw up "—because I did have feelings for you, and they confused me, but in the end, I had to come. Had to ask you for help...help and money, because the pirates are playing games. They're toying with me and I'm scared. Scared of botching this, scared of never seeing my father again, scared that they have all the power and I have none."

She opened her fist, smoothed the creased check, studied the number and sum it represented. "I know you're angry with me, and I know you owe me nothing. I know it's I that owe you, but I need your help, Drakon. At the very least, I need your advice. What do I do now? How do I make sure that they will release my father this time?" Her gaze lifted, met his. "Who is to say that they will ever release him? Who is to say that he's even...he's even..." Her voice drifted off, and she gazed at him, unable to finish the thought.

But she didn't have to finish the thought. "You're afraid he might not be alive," Drakon said, brutally blunt.

She nodded, eyes stinging. "What if he isn't?"

"That's a good question."

"So you see why I need you. I've already given them three million. I can't give them another six without proof, but they refuse to let me speak to him, and I don't know what to do. I'm frightened, Drakon. And overwhelmed. I've been trying to keep it together, but I don't know how to do this—"

"You and your father sing the same tune, don't you?"

She just stared at him, confused. "What does that mean?"

"The only time I hear from you, or your father, is when one of the Copelands needs money. But I'm not a bank, or an ATM machine, and I'm tired of being used."

Morgan struggled to speak. "I never meant to use you, Drakon. And I certainly didn't marry you for money, and I'm ashamed my father asked you to invest in his company, ashamed that he'd put you in that position. I didn't agree with it then, and I'm shattered now that he lost so much of your personal wealth, but he is my father, and I can't leave him in Somalia. It might be acceptable...even fiscally responsible, but it's not morally responsible, not to me. And so I'm here, begging for your help because you are the only one who can help me."

She paused, swallowed, her gaze searching his face, trying to see a hint of softening on his part. "You might not want to hear this right now, Drakon, but you'd do the same if it were your family. I know you...I know who you are, and I know you'd sacrifice everything if you had to."

Drakon looked at her hard, his features harsh, expression shuttered, and then turned away, and walked to the window where he put his hand on the glass, his gaze fixed on the blue horizon. Silence stretched. Morgan waited for him to speak, not wanting to say more, or rush him to a decision, because she knew in her heart, he couldn't tell her no...it'd go against his values, go against his ethics as a man, and a protective Greek male.

But it was hard to wait, and her jaw ached from biting down

so hard, and her stomach churned and her head throbbed, but she had to wait. The ball was in Drakon's court now.

It was a long time before he spoke, and when he did, his voice was pitched so low she had to strain to hear. "I have sacrificed everything for my family," he said roughly. "And it taught me that no good deed goes unpunished."

Her eyes burned, gritty, and her chest squeezed tight with hot emotion. "Please tell me I wasn't the one who taught you that!"

His hand turned into a fist on the window.

Morgan closed her eyes, held her breath, her heart livid with pain. She had loved him…so much…too much….

"I need to think, and want some time," Drakon said, still staring out the window, after another long, tense silence. "Go downstairs. Wait for me there."

CHAPTER THREE

Drakon waited for the bedroom door to close behind Morgan before turning around.

His gut churned with acid and every breath he drew hurt.

He wasn't going to do it. There was no way in hell he'd actually help her free her father. For one—he *hated* her father. For another—Drakon had washed his hands of her. The beard was gone. The vigil was over. Time to move forward.

There was no reason he needed to be involved. No reason to do more than he had. As it was, he'd gone above and beyond the call of duty. He'd given her the money, he'd told her what to do, he'd made it clear that there were those who knew exactly what to do, he'd named the people to call... he'd done everything for her, short of actually dialing Dunamas on his cell phone, and good God, he would not do that.

Drakon stalked back to the bathroom, stared at his reflection, seeing the grim features, the cold, dead eyes, and then suddenly his face dissolved in the mirror and he saw Morgan's instead.

He saw that perfect pale oval with its fine, elegant features, but her loveliness was overshadowed by the worry in her blue eyes, and the dark purple smudges beneath her eyes, and her unnatural pallor. Worse, even here, in the expansive marble bathroom, he could still feel her exhaustion and fatigue.

She'd practically trembled while talking to him, her thin arms and legs still too frail for his liking and he flashed back to that day in New York where he'd spotted her walking out of her shop with Jemma. Morgan might not be sick now, but she didn't look well.

Someone, somewhere should be helping her. Not him... she wasn't his to protect anymore...but there should be someone who could assist her. In an ideal world, there would be someone.

He shook his head, not comfortable with the direction his thoughts were taking him. She's not your problem, he told himself. She's not your responsibility. Not your woman.

Drakon groaned, turned away from the mirror, walked out of the bathroom, to retrieve his phone. He'd make a few calls, check on a few facts, see if he couldn't find someone to work with her, because she'd need someone at her side. Not him, of course, but someone who could offer advice and assistance, or just be a source of support.

Standing outside on his balcony he made a few calls, and then he made a few more, and a few more, and each call was worse than the last.

Morgan Copeland was in trouble.

She'd lost her home, her company, her friends, her reputation. She was a social outcast, *and* she was broke. She was overdrawn in her checking account and she'd maxed out every credit card she owned.

Drakon hung up from his last call and tossed the phone onto the bed.

Dammit.

Dammit.

He was so angry with her....

And so angry with her rarified world for turning on her. She had lost everything. She hadn't been exaggerating.

Morgan was standing in the living room by the enormous wall of windows when Drakon appeared, almost an hour after she'd left him in his bedroom. He'd dressed once again in the off white cashmere V-neck sweater he'd worn earlier, his legs long in the pressed khaki trousers, the sweater smooth over his muscular chest. He'd always had an amazing body, and his perfect build allowed him to wear anything and now with the beard gone she could see his face again and she couldn't look away.

She couldn't call him beautiful, his features were so strong, and his coloring so dark, but he had a sensuality and vitality about him that fascinated her, captivated her. "How long had you been growing that beard?" she asked.

"A long time."

"Years?"

"I'm not here to discuss my beard," he said curtly, crossing the room, walking toward her. "While upstairs I did some research, made a few phone calls, and you did sell your loft. Along with your boutique in SoHo."

Energy crackled around him and Morgan felt her insides jump, tumble. He was so physical, always had been, and the closer he got, the more the tension shifted, growing, building, changing, binding them together the way it always had. The way it always did. "I had to," she said breathlessly, "it was the only way to come up with the money."

"You should have told me immediately that you'd given the Somali pirates ransom money and that they'd failed to release your father."

"I thought you might not have helped me, if you knew...." Her voice faded as Drakon closed the distance between them. He was so alive, so electric, she could almost see little sparks shooting off him. Her heart pounded. Her tummy did another nervous, panicked flip.

She shouldn't have sent away the helicopter. She should have gone while she could. Now it was too late to run. Too late to save herself, and so she stared at him, waited for him, feeling the energy, his energy, that dizzying combination of warmth and heat, light and sparks. This was inevitable. He was inevitable. She could run and run and run, but part of her knew she'd never escape him. She'd run before and yet here she was. Right back where they'd honeymooned, Villa Angelica.

She'd known that coming here, to him, would change everything. Would change her.

It always did.

It already had.

Her legs trembled beneath her. Her heart pounded. Even now, after all these years, she felt almost sick with awareness, need. This chemistry and energy between them was so overwhelming. So consuming. She didn't understand it, and she'd wanted to understand it, if only to help her exorcise him from her heart and her mind.

But all the counselors and doctors and therapists in the world hadn't erased this...him.

Why was Drakon so alive? Why was he more real to her than any other man she'd ever met? After Drakon, after loving Drakon, there could be no one else...he made it impossible for her to even look at anyone else.

He'd reached her, was standing before her, his gaze fierce, intense, as it traveled across her face, making her feel so bare, and naked. Heat bloomed in her skin, blood surging from his close inspection.

"What did you do, Morgan?"

"I don't understand."

"You've sold everything," he added harshly. "You have nothing and even if you get your father back to the United States, you'll still have nothing."

"Not true," she said, locking her knees, afraid she'd collapse, overwhelmed by emotion and memories, overwhelmed by him. She'd been up for two days straight. Hadn't eaten more than a mouthful in that time. She couldn't, knowing she would soon be here, with him again. "I'd have peace of mind."

"Peace of mind?" he demanded. "How can you have peace of mind when you have no home?"

He could mock her, because he didn't know what it was like to lose one's mind. He didn't know that after leaving him, she'd ended up in the hospital and had remained there for far too long. It had been the lowest point in her life, and by far, the darkest part. But she didn't want to think about McLean Hospital now, that was the past, and she had to live in the present, had to stay focused on what was important, like her father. "I did what I had to do."

"You sacrificed your future for your father's, and he doesn't have a future. Your father—*if* alive, *if* released—will be going to prison for the rest of his life. But what will you do while he's in his comfortable, minimum security prison cell, getting three square meals a day? Where will you sleep? What will you eat? How will you get by?"

"I'll figure it out."

"You are so brave and yet foolhardy. Do you ever look before you leap?"

She flashed to Vienna and their wedding and the four weeks of honeymoon, remembering the intense love and need, the hot brilliant desire that had consumed her night and day. She hated to be away from him, hated to wake up without him, hated to breathe without him.

She'd lost herself completely in him. And no, she hadn't looked, hadn't analyzed, hadn't imagined anything beyond that moment when she'd married him and became his.

"No," she answered huskily, lips curving and heart aching. "I just leap, Drakon. Leap and hope I can fly."

If she'd hoped to provoke him, she'd failed. His expression was impassive and he studied her for a long moment from beneath his thick black lashes. "How long has it been since you've spoken to your father?"

"I actually haven't ever spoken to him. My mother did, and just that first day, when they called her to say they had him. Mother summoned us, and told us what had happened, and what the pirates wanted for a ransom."

"How long did she speak to your father?"

"Not long. Just a few words, not much more than that."

"What did he say to her?"

"That his yacht had been seized, his captain killed and he had been abducted, and then the pirates got back on the phone, told her their demands and hung up."

"Has anyone spoken with your father since?"

She shook her head. "No."

"Why not?"

"They won't let us. They say we haven't earned the right."

"But you've given them three million."

Her lips curved bitterly and her gaze lifted to meet his. "I can't sleep at night, knowing I was so stupid and so wasteful. Three million dollars gone! Three million lost forever. It would have been fine if we'd saved my father, but we didn't. I didn't. Instead it's all gone and now I must start over and worse, the ransom has doubled. I'm sick about it, sick that I made such a critical error. I didn't mind liquidating everything to save my father, but it turns out I liquidated everything for nothing—"

"Stop."

"You are right to despise me. I am stupid, stupid, stupid—"

He caught her by the shoulders and gave her a hard shake. "Enough. You didn't know. You didn't understand how the pirates operated, how mercurial they are, how difficult, how unpredictable. You had no way of knowing. There is no handbook on dealing with pirates, so stop torturing yourself."

With every sentence he gave her a little shake until she was thoroughly undone and tears filled her eyes, ridiculous tears that stung and she swiped at them, annoyed, knowing they were from fatigue, not sadness, aware that she was exhausted beyond reason, knowing that what she wanted was

Drakon to kiss her, not shake her, but just because you wanted something didn't mean it was good for you. And Drakon wasn't good for her. She had to remember that.

He saw her tears. His features darkened. "We'll get your father back," he said, his deep voice rumbling through her, his voice as carnal as the rest of him, drawing her into his arms and holding her against his chest, comforting her.

For a moment.

Morgan pulled back, slipping from Drakon's arms, and took several quick steps away to keep from being tempted to return. He'd been so warm. He'd smelled so good. His hard chest, covered in cashmere, had made her want to burrow closer. She'd felt safe there, secure, and yet it was an illusion.

Drakon wasn't safe. He was anything but safe for her.

He watched her make her escape. His jaw jutted, his brow lowered, expression brooding. "We'll get your father back," he said, repeating his promise from a few moments ago. "And we'll do it without giving them another dollar."

She looked up at him, surprised. "How?"

"I know people."

She blinked at him. Of course he knew people—Drakon knew everyone—but could he really free her father without giving the pirates more money? "Is that possible?"

"There are companies...services...that exist just for this purpose."

"I've looked into those companies. They cost millions, and they won't help me. They loathe my father. He represents everything they detest—"

"But they'll work with me."

"Not when they hear who they are to rescue—"

"I own one of the largest shipping companies in the world. No maritime agency would refuse me."

Hope rose up within her, but she didn't trust it, didn't trust anyone or anything anymore. "But you said...you said you wouldn't help me. You said since you'd given me the check—"

"I was wrong. I was being petty. But I can't be petty. You're my wife—" he saw her start to protest and overrode her "—and as long as you are my wife, it's my duty to care for you and your family. It is the vow I made, and a vow I will keep."

"Even though I left you?"

"You left me. I didn't leave you."

Pain flickered through her. "You owe me nothing. I know that. You must know that, too."

"Marriage isn't about keeping score. Life is uneven and frequently unjust and I did not marry you, anticipating only fun and games. I expected there would be challenges, and there have been, far more than I anticipated, but until we are divorced, you are my wife, and the law is the law, and it is my duty to provide for you, to protect you, and I can see I have failed to do both."

She closed her eyes, shattered by his honesty, as well as his sense of responsibility. Drakon was a good man, a fair man, and he deserved a good wife, a wife less highly strung and sensitive...a wife who craved him less, a wife who could live and breathe without him at her side....

Morgan wasn't that woman. Even now she wanted to be back in his arms, to have his mouth on hers, to have him parting her lips, tasting her, filling her, possessing her so completely that the world fell away, leaving just the two of them.

That was her idea of life.

And it was mad and beautiful and impossible and bewitching.

"It's not your fault," she whispered, wrapping her arms around her, wishing she'd needed less talk and tenderness and reassurance. "It's mine. Maybe even my father's. He spoiled me, you know, and it infuriated my mother."

"Your mother did say at our wedding that you were your daddy's little girl."

Morgan's breath caught in her throat and she bit into her bottom lip. "Mother had Tori and Branson and Logan, and yes, I was Daddy's girl, but they were Mother's darlings, and you'd think since she had them living with her, choosing her, she wouldn't mind that I chose to live with Father, but she did."

"What do you mean, they lived with her, and you lived with Daniel? Didn't you all live together?"

Morgan shook her head. "Mother and Father lived apart most of the time. They'd put on a show for everyone else— united front for the public, always throwing big parties for the holidays or special occasions…Christmas party, New Year's party, birthdays and anniversaries. But behind closed doors, they could barely tolerate each other and were almost never in the same place at the same time, unless there was a photo shoot, or reporter about. Mother loved being in the society columns, loved having our lavish, privileged lifestyle featured in glossy magazines. She liked being envied, enjoyed her place in the sun. Father was different. He hadn't grown up with money like Mother, and wasn't comfortable in the spotlight. He lived far more quietly…he and I, and Jemma, when she joined us. We'd go to these small neighborhood restaurants and they weren't trendy in the least. We loved our Mexican food and Greek food and Indian food and maybe once every week or two, we'd send out for Chinese food. After dinner, once my homework was done, we'd watch television in the evening…we had our favorite show. We had our routines. It was lovely. He was lovely. And ordinary." She looked up at Drakon, sorrow in her eyes. "But the world now won't ever know that man, or allow him to be that man. In their eyes, he's a greedy selfish hateful man, but he wasn't. He really wasn't—" She broke off, drew a deep breath and then another.

"Mother used to say I was a demanding little girl, and she hated that Father humored me. She said he spoiled me by taking me everywhere with him, and turning me into his shadow. Apparently that's why I became so clingy with you. I shifted my attachment from my father onto you. But what a horrible thing for you...to be saddled with a wife who can't be happy on her own—"

"You're talking nonsense, Morgan—"

"No, it's true."

"Well, I don't buy it. I was never saddled with you, nor did I ever feel encumbered by you. I'm a man. I do as I please and I married you because I chose you, and I stayed married to you because I chose to, and that's all there is to it."

She looked away, giving him her profile. It was such a beautiful profile. Delicate. Elegant. The long, black eyelashes, the sweep of cheekbone, the small straight nose, the strong chin, above an impossibly long neck. The Copeland girls were all stunning young women, but there was something ethereal about Morgan...something mysterious.

"You're exhausted," he added. "I can see you're not eating or sleeping and that must change. I will not have you become skin and bones again. While you're here, you will sit and eat real meals, and rest, and allow me to worry about things. I may not have been the patient and affectionate husband you wanted, but I'm good at managing chaos, and I'm damn good at dealing with pirates."

He didn't know what he expected, but he didn't expect her to suddenly smile at him, the first smile he'd seen from her since she arrived, and it was radiant, angelic, starting in her stunning blue eyes and curving her lips and making her lovely face come alive.

For a moment he could only look at her, and appreciate her. She was like the sun and she glowed, vital, beautiful, and he remembered that first night in Vienna when she'd turned and looked at him, her blue eyes dancing, mischief playing at her mouth, and then she'd spotted him, her eyes meeting his, and her smile had faded, and she'd become shy.

She'd blushed and turned away but then she'd peek over her shoulder at him again and again and by the end of the ball he knew he would have her. She was his. She would always be his. Thank God she'd felt the same way. It would have created an international scandal if he'd had to kidnap her and drag her off to Greece, an unwilling bride.

"I am happy to allow you to take the lead when it comes to the pirates," she said, her smile slowly dying, "and you may manage them, but Drakon, you mustn't try to manage me. I won't be managed. I've had enough of that these past five years."

Drakon frowned, sensing that there was a great deal she wasn't saying, a great deal he wouldn't like hearing, and he wanted to ask her questions, hard questions, but now wasn't the time, not when she was so fragile and fatigued. There would be time for all his questions later, time to learn just what had dismantled his marriage, and who and what had been managing her, but he could do that when she wasn't trembling with exhaustion and with dark purple circles shadowing her eyes.

"I'm concerned about you," he said flatly.

"There's been a lot of stress lately."

He didn't doubt that, and it crossed his mind that if he'd been a real husband, and a more selfless man, he would have gone to Morgan, and offered her support or assistance before it'd come to this. Instead, he, like the rest of the world, had followed the Copeland family crisis from afar, reading about the latest humiliation or legal move in the media, and doing nothing.

"I can see that, but you'll be of no use to your father, if you fall apart yourself," he said. "I'll make some calls and the staff can prepare us a late lunch—"

"Do we really need lunch?"

"Yes, we do. And while I understand time is of the essence, not eating will only make things worse. We need clear

heads and fierce resolve, and that won't happen if we're fainting on our feet."

Morgan suddenly laughed and she shook her head, once
again giving him a glimpse of the Morgan he'd married…
young and vivacious and full of laughter and passion. "You
keep using 'we,' when we both know you mean me." She
paused and her gaze lifted, her eyes meeting his. "But I do
rather like the image of you fainting on your feet."

His gaze met hers and held and it was all he could do to
keep from reaching for her. He wanted her. Still wanted her
more than he'd wanted anyone or anything. "Of course you
would," he said roughly. "You're a wicked woman and you
deserve to be—"

Drakon broke off abruptly, balling his hands into fists
and he realized how close he'd come to teasing her the way
he'd once teased her, promising her punishment, which was
merely foreplay to make her hot, to make her wet, to make
her shudder with pleasure.

It used to give him such pleasure that he brought her pleasure. He wasn't good at saying all the right words, so he
used his body to say how much he adored her, how much he
desired her, how much he cherished her and would always
cherish her.

But only now did he know she'd hated the way he'd plea-
sured her.

That she'd been disgusted—

"Don't," she whispered, reaching out to him, her hand settling on his arm. "Don't do that, don't. I know what you're
thinking, and I'm sorry. I shouldn't have said what I did,
shouldn't have said it how I did. It was wrong. I was wrong.
I was upset."

His body hardened instantly at her touch, and he glanced
down at her hand where it clung to his forearm. He could feel
her warmth through the softness of the cashmere, and the

press of her fingers, and it was nothing at all, and yet it was everything, too. Nothing and everything at the same time.

He looked away from her hand, up into her eyes, angry with her all over again, but also angry with himself. How could he have not known how she felt? How could he have not realized that she didn't enjoy...him...them?

"Rest assured that I will not take advantage of you while you are here," he said, trying to ease some of the tension rippling through him. "You are safe in the villa," he continued, hating that he suddenly felt like a monster. He wasn't a monster. Not even close. It's true he could be ruthless in business, and he had a reputation for being a fierce negotiator, a brilliant strategist, an analytical executive, as well as a demanding boss, but that didn't make him an ogre and he'd never knowingly hurt a woman, much less his wife. "You are safe from me."

"Drakon."

"I'll have your bag taken up to the Angelica Suite," he said. "It's the second master suite, on the third floor, the suite one with the frescoed ceiling."

"I remember it."

"It's in the opposite wing of where I'm staying but it should give you privacy and I think you'll find it quite comfortable. I can show you the way now."

"There's no need to take me there," she said hoarsely. "I remember the suite."

"Fine. Then I'll let you find your way, and as I have quite a few things to do, I'll eat as I work, and I'll have a light lunch sent to you in your room, but we'll need to meet later so I can fill you in on the arrangements I've been able to make for your father."

Morgan was glad to escape to her room, desperate to get away from Drakon and that intense physical awareness of him....

She'd hurt him. What she'd said earlier, about their sex

life, about their marriage, it'd hurt him terribly and she felt guilty and sorry. So very sorry since she knew Drakon would never do anything to hurt her. He'd always been so protective of her but he was also so very physical, so carnal and sexual and she was a little afraid of it. And him. Not when she was with him, making love to him, but later, when he was gone, separated from her. It was then that she analyzed their relationship, and what they did and how they did it and how little control she had with him.

It frightened her that she lost control with him.

Frightened her that he had so much power and she had so little.

It had niggled at her during their honeymoon, but their picnics and dinners out and the afternoon trips on his yacht were so fun and romantic that she could almost forget how fierce and shattering the sex was when he was charming and attentive and affectionate. But in Athens when he disappeared into his work life, his real life, the raw nature of their sex life struck her as ugly, and she became ugly and it all began to unravel, very, very quickly.

Upstairs in her suite, Morgan barely had time to open the two sets of French doors before a knock sounded on the outer bedroom door, letting her know her overnight bag had arrived. She thanked the housemaid and then returned to the first of the two generous balconies with the stunning view.

She had never tired of this view. She couldn't imagine how anyone could tire of it.

The Amalfi Coast's intense blues and greens contrasted by rugged rock had inspired her very first jewelry collection. She'd worked with polished labradorite, blue chalcedony, pāua shell, lapis lazuli and Chinese turquoise, stones she'd acquired on two extensive shopping trips through Southeast Asia, from Hong Kong to Singapore to Bali.

It'd been a three-month shopping expedition that big sister

Tori had accompanied her on for the first month, and then Logan came for the second month, and Jemma for the third.

By the time Morgan returned to New York, she'd filled two enormous trunks of stones and had a briefcase and laptop full of sketches and the first orders from Neiman Marcus and Bergdorf Goodman. The designs were pure fantasy—a stunning collection of statement-making collars, cuffs and drop earrings—and had cost her a fortune in stone. It had tested her ability to execute her ideas, but had ended up being worth every stress and struggle as the Amalfi Collection turned out to be a huge success, generating significant media attention, as well as the attention of every fashion designer and fashion publicist of note, never mind the starlets, celebrities and socialites who all wanted a Morgan Copeland statement piece.

Morgan's second collection, Jasper Ice, had been inspired by her love of the Canadian Rockies and ski trips to Banff and Lake Louise. The collection was something that an ice princess in a frozen tundra would wear—frosty and shimmering pieces in white, silver, blush, beige and pale gold. The second collection did almost as well as the first, and garnered even more media with mentions in virtually every fashion magazine in North America, Europe and Australia, and then photographed on celebrities and young royals, like the Saudi princess who had worn a gorgeous pink diamond cuff for her wedding.

Morgan was glad Jasper Ice did well, but the cool, frozen beauty of the collection was too much like her numb emotional state, when she'd been so fiercely, frantically alive and in love with Drakon Xanthis.

Drakon, though, was the last person she wanted to think of, especially when she was enjoying the heady rush of success, and for a while she had been very good at blocking him out of her mind, but then one October day, she had been walking with Jemma to lunch and she had spotted a man in a limousine. He'd had a beard and his hair was long but his eyes reminded her so much of Drakon that for a moment she thought it was him.

She had kept walking, thinking she'd escaped, but then a block away from her shop, she'd had to stop, lean against a building and fight for air.

She'd felt like she was having a heart attack. Her chest hurt, the muscles seizing, and she couldn't breathe, couldn't get air, couldn't even speak. She opened her mouth, stared at Jemma, wanting, needing help, but she couldn't make a sound. Then everything went black.

When she woke up, she'd been in an ambulance, and then when she woke again, she was in a bed in the emergency room. She'd spent the next ten days in the hospital, six in ICU, being seen by cardiac specialists. The specialists explained that her extreme weight loss had damaged her heart, and they warned her that if she didn't make immediate and drastic changes, she could die of heart failure.

But Morgan hadn't been dieting. She didn't want to lose weight. She had just found it impossible to eat when her heart was broken. But she wasn't a fool, she understood the gravity of her situation, and recognized she was in trouble.

During the day they'd fed her special shakes and meals and at night she'd dreamed of Drakon, and the dreams had been so vivid and intense that she'd woke desperate each morning to actually see him. She made the mistake of telling Logan that she was dreaming about Drakon every night, and Logan had told their mother, who then told the doctors, and before Morgan knew it, the psychiatrists were back with their pills and questions and notepads.

Did she understand the difference between reality and fantasy?

Did she understand the meaning of wish fulfillment?

Did she want to die?

It would have been puzzling if she hadn't been through all this before at McLean Hospital in Massachusetts, and then at the Wallace Home for a year after that. But she had been through it before so she found the doctors with their clip-boards and questions and colorful assortment of pills annoy-ing and even somewhat amusing.

She'd refused the pills. She'd answered some questions. She'd refused to answer others.

She wasn't sick or crazy this time. She was just pushing herself too hard, working too many hours, not eating and sleeping enough.

Morgan had promised her medical team and her family she'd slow down, and eat better, and sleep more and enjoy life more, and for the next two plus years she did. She began to take vacations, joining her sisters for long holidays at the family's Caribbean island, or skiing in Sun Valley or Cham-onix, and sometimes she just went off on her own, visiting exotic locations for inspiration for her jewelry designs.

She'd also learned her lesson. She couldn't, wouldn't, men-tion Drakon again.

Those ten days in the hospital, and her vivid, shattering dreams at night, had inspired her third collection, the Black Prince, a glamorous, dramatic collection built of ruby hues—garnets, red spinels, pink sapphires, diamonds, pave garnets, watermelon tourmaline, pink tourmaline. The collection was a tribute to her brief marriage and the years that followed, mad love, accompanied by mad grief. In her imagination, the Black Prince was Drakon, and the bloodred jewels rep-resented her heart, which she'd cut and handed to him, while the pink sapphires and delicate tourmalines were the tears she'd cried leaving him.

But, of course, she had to keep that inspiration to herself, and so she came up with a more acceptable story for the public, claiming that her newest collection was inspired by the Black Prince's ruby, a 170-carat red spinel once worn in Henry V's battle helmet.

The collection was romantic and over-the-top and wildly

passionate, and early feedback had seemed promising with orders pouring in for the large rings, and jeweled cuffs, and stunning pendulum necklaces made of eye-popping pale pink tourmaline—but then a week before the official launch of her collection, news of the Michael Amery scandal broke and she knew she was in trouble. It was too late to pull any of her ads, or change the focus of the marketing for her latest Morgan Copeland collection.

It was absolutely the wrong collection to be launched in the middle of a scandal implicating Daniel Copeland, and thereby tarnishing the Copeland name. The Black Prince Collection had been over-the-top even at conception, and the finished pieces were sensual and emotional, extravagant and dramatic, and at any other time, the press and fashion darlings would have embraced her boldness, but in the wake of the scandal where hundreds of thousands of people had been robbed by Michael Amery and Daniel Copeland, the media turned on her, criticizing her for being insensitive and hopelessly out of touch with mainstream America. One critic went so far as to compare her to Marie Antoinette, saying that the Black Prince Collection was as "frivolous and useless" as Morgan Copeland herself.

Morgan had tried to prepare herself for the worst, but the viciousness of the criticism, and the weeks of vitriolic attacks, had been unending. Her brother, Branson, a media magnate residing in London, had sent her an email early on, advising her to avoid the press, and to not read the things being written about her. But she did read them. She couldn't seem to help herself.

In the fallout following the Amery Ponzi scandal, the orders that had been placed for her lush Black Prince Collection were canceled, and stores that had trumpeted her earlier collections quietly returned her remaining pieces and closed their accounts with her. No one wanted to carry anything with the Copeland name. No one wanted to have an association with her.

It was crushing, financially and psychologically. She'd invested hundreds of thousands of dollars into the stones, as well as thousands and thousands into the labor, and thousands more into the marketing and sales. The entire collection was a bust, as was her business.

Fortunately, there was no time to wallow in self-pity. The phone call from Northern Africa, alerting her that her father had been kidnapped, had forced her to prioritize issues. She could grieve the loss of her business later. Now, she had to focus on her father.

And yet...standing here, on the balcony, with the bright sun glittering on the sapphire water, Morgan knew she wouldn't have had any success as a designer, or any confidence in her creative ability, if it hadn't been for her honeymoon here in this villa.

And Drakon.

But that went without saying.

CHAPTER FOUR

MORGAN HAD ONLY packed her traveling clothes and the one blue linen top and skirt she'd changed into after arriving in Naples, and so before lunch arrived, she slipped into her comfortable tracksuit to eat her lunch on the balcony before taking a nap. She hadn't meant to sleep the afternoon away but she loved the breeze from the open doors and how it fluttered the long linen curtains and carried the scents of wisteria and roses and lemon blossoms.

She slept for hours in the large bed with the fluffy duvet and the down pillows all covered in the softest of linens. The Italians knew how to make decadent linens and it was here on her honeymoon that she'd come to appreciate cool, smooth sheets and lazy afternoon naps. She'd fall asleep in Drakon's arms after making love and wake in his arms and make love yet again and it was all so sensual, so indulgent. It had been pure fantasy.

She'd dreamed of Drakon while she slept, dreamed they were still together, still happy, and parents of a beautiful baby girl. Waking, Morgan reached for Drakon, her hand slipping sleepily across the duvet, only to discover that the other side of her big bed was empty, cool, the covers undisturbed. Rolling onto her side, she realized it was just a dream. Yet more fantasy.

Tears stung her eyes and her heart felt wrenched, and the heartbreak of losing Drakon felt as real as it had five years ago, when her family had insisted she go to McLean Hospital instead of return to Drakon in Greece.

You're not well. This isn't healthy. You're not healthy. You're too desperate. This is insanity. You're losing your mind... .

Her throat swelled closed and her chest ached and she bit into her lip to keep the memories at bay.

If she hadn't left Drakon they probably would have children now. Babies...toddlers...little boys and girls...

She'd wanted a family with him, but once in Greece Drakon had become a stranger and she had feared they were turning into her own parents: distant, silent, destined to live separate lives.

She couldn't do it. Couldn't be like her parents. Wouldn't raise children in such an unhealthy, unsuitable environment.

Stop thinking about it, she told herself, flipping the covers back and leaving the bed to bathe before dinner. In her grand bathroom with the soaring frescoed ceiling and the warm cream-and-terra-cotta marble, she took a long soak in the deep tub before returning to the bedroom to put her tired linen skirt and blouse back on. But in the bedroom the crumpled blue skirt and blouse were gone and in their place was a huge open Louis Vuitton trunk sitting on the bench at the foot of the bed.

She recognized the elegant taupe-and-cream trunk—it was part of the luggage set her father had given her before her wedding and it was filled with clothes. Her clothes, her shoes, her jewelry, all from the Athens villa. Drakon must have sent for them. It was a thoughtful gesture and she was grateful for clean clothes and something fresh to wear, but it was painful seeing her beautiful wardrobe...so very extravagant, so much couture. So much money invested in a couple dozen dresses and blouses and trousers. Thousands more in shoes and purses.

Morgan sorted through the sundresses and evening dresses

and chic tunics and caftans. Her sisters were far more fash-
ionable than she was, and constantly pushing her to be a bit
more trendy, but Morgan liked to be comfortable and loved
floaty dresses that skimmed her body rather than hug every
curve, but she needed something more fitted tonight, something to keep her together because she was so close to falling apart.

She settled on a white eyelet dress with a boned corset and
small puffy sleeves that made her feel like a Gypsy, and she
added gold hoop earrings and a coral red shawl worn loosely
around her shoulders. Morgan didn't wear a lot of makeup
and applied just a hint of color to her cheeks and lips, a little
concealer to soften the circles that remained beneath her eyes
and then a bit of mascara because it gave her confidence.

The sun was just starting to set as she headed downstairs.
She remembered her way to the dining room, but one of the
villa staff was on hand at the foot of the stairs to escort her
there. Before she'd even entered the dining room she spotted Drakon on the patio, through the dining room's open
doors. He was outside, leaning against the iron railing, talking on the phone.

She hesitated before joining him, content for a moment to
just look at him while he was preoccupied.

He'd changed from the cashmere sweater to a white linen
shirt and a pair of jeans for dinner. His choice in wardrobe
surprised her.

Jeans.

She'd never seen him wear jeans before, and these weren't
fancy European denim jeans, but the faded American Levi's
style and they looked amazing on him. The jeans were old
and worn and they outlined Drakon's strong thighs and
hugged his hard butt and made her look a little too long at
the button fly that covered his impressive masculine parts.

How odd this new Drakon was, so different from the sophisticated, polished man she'd remembered all these years

ago. His beard and long hair might be gone, but he still wasn't the Drakon of old. He was someone else, someone new, and that kept taking her by surprise.

The Drakon she'd married had been an incredibly successful man aware of his power, his wealth, his stature. He'd liked Morgan to dress up, to wear beautiful clothes, to be seen in the best of everything, and Drakon himself dressed accordingly. He wouldn't have ever worn a simple white linen shirt halfway unbuttoned to show off his bronze muscular chest. He'd been too controlled, too tightly wound, while this man...he oozed recklessness. And sex.

Drakon had always had an amazing body, but this new one was even stronger and more fit now and Morgan swallowed hard, hating to admit it, but she was fascinated by him. Fascinated and a little bit turned on, which wasn't at all appropriate given the situation, especially considering how Drakon had promised not to touch her....

Drakon suddenly turned, and looked straight at her, his amber gaze meeting hers through the open door. Despite everything, heat flickered in his eyes and she swallowed hard again, even as she blushed hotly, aware that she'd been caught staring.

Nervous, she squared her shoulders and briskly crossed the dining room before stepping outside onto the patio. Drakon had just ended his call as she joined him outside and he slipped the phone into the front pocket of his jeans.

Those damn faded jeans that lovingly outlined his very male body.

There was no reason a Greek shipping magnate needed a body like that. It was decadent for a man who already had so much. His body was beautiful. Sexual. Sinful. He knew how to use it, too, especially those lean hard hips. Never mind his skillful fingers, lips and tongue.

"Hope I didn't keep you waiting long," he said.

Cheeks hot, insides flip-flopping, she reluctantly dragged

her gaze from his button fly up to his face with its newly shaven jaw and square chin. "No," she murmured, almost missing the dark thick beard and long hair. When she'd first arrived, he'd looked so primitive and primal. So undeniably male that she wouldn't have been surprised if he'd pushed her up against the wall and taken her there.

Perhaps a little part of her wished he had.

Instead he'd vowed to stay away from her, and she knew Drakon took his vows seriously. Was it so wrong of her to wish he'd kissed her properly before he'd made that vow? Was it wrong to crave his skin even though he'd made the vow already?

Just thinking of his skin made her glance at his chest, at that broad expanse of hard muscle, and her body reacted, her inner thighs tightening, clenching, while her lower belly ached with emptiness. She hadn't been honest with him. She had loved to make love with him, loved the way he felt inside of her, his body buried deeply between her thighs and how he'd draw back before thrusting back in, over and over until she raked her nails across his shoulders and gripped his arms and arched under him, crying his name.

And just remembering, she could almost feel the weight of him now, his arms stretching her arms above her head, his hands circling her wrists, his chest pressed to her breasts. He'd thrust his tongue into her mouth even as his hard, hot body thrust into hers, burying himself so deeply she couldn't think, feel, want anything but Drakon.

Drakon.

And now she was here with him. Finally. After all these years.

Morgan, it's not going to happen, she told herself. He's letting you go. You're moving on. There will be no sex against the wall, or sex on the floor, or sex on the small dining table painted gold and rose with the lush sunset.

But wouldn't it feel good? another little voice whispered.

Of course it'd feel good. Everything with Drakon had felt good. Sex wasn't the problem. It was the distance after the sex that was.

"Something to drink?" he asked, gesturing to the bar set up in the corner and filled with dozens of bottles with colorful labels. "I can make you a mixed drink, or pour you a glass of wine."

"A glass of wine," she said, as a breeze blew in from the sea, and caught at her hair, teasing a dark tendril.

"Red or white?"

"Doesn't matter. You choose."

He poured her a glass of red wine. "Were you able to sleep?" he asked, handing her the goblet, and their fingers brushed.

A frisson of pleasure rushed through her at the brief touch. Her pulse quickened and she had to exhale slowly, needing to calm herself, settle herself. She couldn't lose focus, had to remember why she was here. Her father. Her father, who was in so much danger. "Yes," she said, her voice pitched low, husky with a desire she could barely master, never mind hide.

Drakon stiffened at the sudden spike of awareness. Morgan practically hummed with tension, her slim figure taut, energy snapping and crackling around her. It was hot and electric, she was hot and electric, and he knew if he reached for her, touched her, she'd let him. She wanted him. Morgan had been right about the physical side of their relationship. There was plenty of heat...intense chemistry...but she'd been the one that brought the fire to their relationship. She'd brought it out in him. He'd enjoyed sex with other women, but with her, it wasn't just sex. It was love. And he'd never loved a woman before her. He'd liked them, admired them, enjoyed them...but had never loved, not the way he loved her, and he was quite sure he would never love any woman this way again.

"For hours," she added, blushing, her voice still husky. "It was lovely. But then, I always sleep well here."

"It's the air, I think," he said. "You look beautiful, by the way," he said.

Her cheeks turned pink and her blue eyes glowed with pleasure. She looked surprised, touched. His beautiful woman. Part of him wanted to shake her, kiss her, make her his again, and another part of him wanted to send her away forever.

"Thank you for sending for my clothes," she said, fighting the same tendril of hair, the one the breeze loved to tease. "That was very kind of you."

"Not kind, just practical," he answered. "Since you're not returning to Ekali, there's no point keeping your things at the villa there anymore. Which reminds me, I have another trunk with your winter clothes and ski things ready to go home with you when you leave for New York. It's in one of the storage rooms downstairs. Didn't see any reason to drag it up three flights of stairs only to drag it down again in a few days.

A shadow passed across her face. "Is that how long you think I need to be here?"

"We'll know better once Rowan arrives. I expect him in late tonight or early tomorrow."

"Rowan?"

"Rowan Argyros, from Dunamas Maritime Intelligence. He's the one I work with when my ships have been seized. His headquarters are in London, but when I phoned him this afternoon I learned that he's in Los Angeles and he's promised to fly out this afternoon."

"But if you are a maritime piracy expert, why do you need outside help?"

"Because while I know shipping, and I've becoming quite knowledgeable about counter-piracy, it takes more than money to free a seized ship, or crew being held hostage. It takes a team of experts, as well as information, strategy and decisive action, and in your father's case, it will take extraordinary action. As you can imagine, it's crucial to do everything exactly right. There is no room for error in something like this. Even a small mistake could cost his life."

She paled. "Perhaps it's too dangerous."

"Rowan won't act unless he's sure of a positive outcome."

He watched her bite nervously into her lower lip and his gaze focused on that soft bottom lip. For a few seconds, he could think of nothing but her mouth. He loved the shape, the color, the softness of it. Always had. Her lips were full and a tender pink that made him think of lush, ripe summer fruit—sweet strawberries and cherries and juicy watermelon.

"We don't even know if my father is alive," she said after a moment, looking up into his eyes.

He knew from her expression that she was looking for reassurance, but he couldn't give it, not yet, not until Rowan had finished his intelligence work. And yet at the same time, there was no reason to alarm her. Information would be coming soon. Until then, they had to be positive. "We don't know very much about his condition at the moment, but I think it's important to focus on the best outcome, not the worst."

"When do you think this...Rowan...will have news for us?"

"I expect he'll have information when he arrives."

Morgan's eyes searched his again and her worry and fear were tangible and he fought the impulse to reach for her, comfort her, especially when she was so close he could feel her warmth and smell her light, delicate fragrance, a heady mix of perfume and her skin.

"It's difficult waiting," she said softly, the tip of her tongue touching her upper lip. "Difficult to be calm and patient in the face of so much unknown."

The glimpse of her pink tongue made him instantly hard. He wanted her so much, couldn't imagine not wanting her. It was torture being this close and yet not being able to kiss her, hold her, and he hardened all over again at the thought of kissing her, and tasting her and running his tongue across the seam of her lips.

He'd been with no one since Morgan left. For five years he'd gone without a woman, gone without closeness, intimacy, gone without even a kiss, and he suddenly felt starved. Ravenous. Like a man possessed. He needed her. She was his. His wife, his woman—

Drakon stopped himself. He couldn't go there, couldn't think of her like that. She might be his legally, but the relationship itself was over. "But that is life," he said grimly. "It is nothing but the unknown."

His staff appeared on the patio, lighting candles and sconces, including the heavy silver candelabra on the round white-linen covered table. "It appears dinner is ready," he added, glad for the diversion. "Shall we sit?"

Morgan realized with a start that the sun had dropped significantly and now hung just above the sea, streaking the horizon red, rose and gold. It would be a stunning sunset and they'd be here on the patio to see it. "Yes, please," she said, moving toward the table, but Drakon was already there, holding a chair for her.

She felt the electric shock as she sat down, her shoulder briefly touching his chest, and then his fingers brushing across the back of her bare arm. Her shawl had slipped into the crook of her elbow and the unexpected sensation of his skin on hers made her breath catch in her throat and she held the air bottled in her lungs as she pressed her knees tightly together, feeling the hot lick of desire and knowing she had to fight it.

"It will be a gorgeous sunset," she said, determined to think of other things than the useless dampness between her thighs and the coiling in her belly that made her feel so empty and achy.

His amber gaze met hers, and the warm tawny depths were piercing, penetrating, and it crossed her mind that he *knew.*

He knew how she felt, he knew she wanted him, and it was suddenly too much...being here, alone with him.

"Must grab my camera," she said, leaping to her feet. "Such an incredible sunset."

She rushed off, up to her room, where she dug through her things and located her phone, which was also her camera, but didn't return to the dining room immediately, needing the time to calm herself and pull her frayed nerves back together.

He's always done this to you, she lectured herself. *He seduced you with his eyes long before he ever touched you, but that doesn't mean anything. It's lust. He's good at sex. That doesn't mean he should be your husband.*

Morgan returned downstairs, head high. As she approached the patio through the dining room, the sunset bathed the patio in soft golden light. The small, round dining table seemed to float above the shimmering green tiles on the patio. The same green tiles extended all the way into the dining room and from the kitchen she caught a whiff of the most delicious aromas—tomato and onion, garlic, olive oil, herbs—even as the breeze rustled her skirts, tugging at her air, whispering over her skin.

So much light and color and sound.

So much sensation. So much emotion. It was wonderful and terrible...bittersweet. Drakon and Villa Angelica had made her feel alive again.

Drakon rose as she stepped out onto the patio. "The sun is almost gone," he said, holding her chair for her.

She glanced out at the sea, and he was right. The bright red ball of sun had disappeared into the water. "I did miss it," she said, hoping she sounded properly regretful as she sat back down.

"Maybe next time," he said, with mock sympathy.

She looked up at him and then away, aware that he was playing her game with her. Pretending she'd wanted a photo when they both knew she just needed to escape him.

"I'll have to keep my phone close by," she said, reaching for her water glass and taking a quick sip.

His gaze collided with hers and then held, his expression one of lazy amusement. "Photos really help one remember things."

She felt herself grow warm. "I have a purely professional interest in the scenery."

"Is that so?"

She hated the way one of his black eyebrows lifted. Hated that curl of his lips. It was sardonic, but also quite sexy, and she was sure he knew it. "I use them for inspiration, not souvenirs," she said coolly, wanting to squash him, and his amusement. There was no reason for him to take pleasure in her discomfiture. No reason for him to act superior.

"Interesting," he drawled, and Morgan had to restrain herself from kicking him beneath the table because she knew he didn't mean it. And he didn't believe her. He probably was sitting there arrogantly thinking she was completely hung up on him…and imagining she was obsessing about having great sex with him…which was ludicrous because she wasn't thinking about having great sex with him anymore. At least not when she was talking about the scenery and inspiration.

"I use the inspiration for my work," she said defiantly, not even sure why she was getting so upset. "But you probably don't consider it work. You probably think it's silly. Superficial."

"I never said that."

"Perhaps you didn't say it, but you think it. You know you do."

"I find it interesting that you feel compelled to put words into my mouth."

His ability to be so calm and detached when she was feeling so emotional made her even more emotional. She leaned toward him. "Surely you've wondered what drove you to marry a flighty woman like me...a woman so preoccupied with frivolous things."

"Are you flighty?"

"You must think so."

He leaned forward, too, closing the distance between them. "I'm not asking you to tell me what I think. I'm asking you—are you flighty?"

Her chin jerked up. "No."

"Are you preoccupied with frivolous things?" he persisted.

Her cheeks burned hot and her eyes felt gritty. "No."

"So you're not flighty or frivolous?"

"No."

His eyes narrowed. "Then why would I think you are?"

She had to close her eyes, overwhelmed by pain and the wave of grief that swept over her.

"Morgan?"

She gave her head a small shake, refusing to open her eyes until she was sure they were perfectly dry. "I am sorry," she said huskily. "You deserved better than me."

"And I'd like to hear more about your jewelry and your ideas, unless you're determined to hold onto this bizarre fantasy of yours that I don't care for you or what's going on inside that beautiful, but complicated head."

She suddenly seethed with anger. Why was he so interested in her thoughts now, when he hadn't been interested in anything but her body when they'd lived together? "I loved what I did," she said shortly. "I was really proud of my work, and I am still proud of those three collections."

She glared at him, waiting for him to speak, but he simply sat back in his chair and looked at her, and let the silence grow, expand and threaten to take over.

The silence was beginning to feel uncomfortable and he was examining her a little too closely. She felt herself grow warm, too warm. "They were jewelry, yes," she said, rushing now to fill the silence, "but they were also miniature works of art, and each collection had a theme and each individual piece told a story."

"And what were those stories?"

"Life and death, love and loss, hope and despair..." Her voice faded, and she looked away, heart aching, because the collections had really been about him, them, their brief fierce love that became so very dangerous and destructive.

"I liked them all, but my favorite collection was your last one. The one you called a failure."

Her head jerked up and she had to blink hard to keep tears from welling up. "You're familiar with my three collections?"

"But of course."

"And you liked my designs?"

"You have such a unique vision. I admired your work very much."

She exhaled slowly, surprised, touched, grateful. "Thank you."

"I was proud of you, my wife. I still am."

The tears she'd been fighting filled her eyes and she didn't know what affected her more—his words or his touch. "My short-lived career," she said, struggling to speak, trying to sound light, mocking, but it had hurt, closing her business. She'd truly loved her work. Had found so much joy in her work and designs.

He caught one of her tears before it could fall. "I don't think it's over. I think you're in the middle of a transition period, and it may feel like death, but it's just change."

"Well, death certainly is a change," she answered, deadpan, flashing him a crooked smile, thinking she liked it when Drakon talked to her. She'd always liked his perspective on things. She found it—him—reassuring, and for her, this is how she connected to him. Through words. Language. Ideas.

If only they'd had more of this—time and conversation—perhaps she wouldn't have felt so lost in Greece. Perhaps they'd still be together now.

He suddenly reached out and stroked her cheek with his thumb, making her heart turn over once again.

"I liked it when you smiled a moment ago," he said gruffly, his amber gaze warm as he looked at her. "I have a feeling you don't smile much anymore."

For a moment she didn't speak, she couldn't, her heart in her mouth and her chest filled with hot emotion.

She was still so drawn to him, still so in love with him. But there was no relationship anymore. They were mostly definitely done—finished. No turning back.

He was helping her because she needed help, but that was all. She had to remember what was important—her father and securing his release—and not let herself get caught up in the physical again because the physical was maddening, disorienting and so incredibly addictive. She hadn't known she had such an addictive personality, not until she'd fell for Drakon.

"There hasn't been a great deal to smile about in the past few months," she said quietly. "Everything has been so grim and overwhelming, but just being here, having your support, gives me hope. If you hadn't agreed to help me, I don't know what I would have done. I'm so very grateful—"

"Your father's not home yet."

"But with your help, he soon will be."

"Careful, my love. You can't say that. You don't know that."

She averted her head and blinked hard, gazing out across the water that had darkened to purple beneath a lavender sky. The first stars were appearing and the moon was far away, just a little crescent of white.

"I'm not saying that it's hopeless," Drakon said. "Just that there is still a great deal we do not know yet."

"I understand. I do."

CHAPTER FIVE

MORGAN PASSED ON coffee and returned to her room, finding it far too painful to sit across from Drakon and look at him, and be so close to him, and yet not be part of his life anymore. Better to return to her suite and pace the floor in privacy, where he couldn't read her face or know how confused she felt.

How could she still want him so much even now? How could she want him when she knew how dangerous he was for her?

She needed to go home, back to New York, back to her family. There was no reason to remain here. Surely this man, Rowan whatever-his-name-was, from Dunamas Intelligence, didn't need her here for his work. He could email her, or call, when he had news....

Morgan nearly returned downstairs to tell Drakon she wanted to leave tonight, that she insisted on leaving tonight, but as she opened her door she realized how ridiculous she'd sound, demanding to go just when Rowan was set to arrive. No, she needed to calm down. She was being foolish. As well as irrational. Drakon wouldn't hurt her. He wasn't going to destroy her. She just needed to keep her head, and not let him anywhere close to her body.

Morgan went to bed, thinking she'd be too wound up to sleep, but she did finally sleep and then woke up early, her room filled with dazzling morning sunlight. After showering, she dressed simply in slim white slacks and one of her favorite colorful tunics and headed downstairs to see if she could get a coffee.

One of the maids gestured to the breakfast room, which was already set for two. Morgan shook her head. "Just coffee," she said, unable to stomach the idea of another meal with Drakon. "An Americano with milk. Latte," she added. "But nothing to eat."

The maid didn't understand and gestured again to the pretty table with its cheerful yellow and blue linens and smiled winningly.

"No, no. Just coffee. Take away." Morgan frowned, wondering why she couldn't seem to remember a single word of Italian. She used to know a little bit, but her brain wasn't working this morning. She was drawing a total blank.

The maid smiled. "Coffee. Americano, *si. Prego.*" And she gestured to the table once more.

Morgan gave up and sat down at the table, needing coffee more than argument. She ended up having breakfast alone and enjoyed her warm pastries and juice and strong hot coffee, which she laced with milk.

The sun poured in through the tall leaded windows, and light dappled the table, shining on the blue water glasses and casting prisms of delicate blue on the white plaster walls.

Morgan studied the patches of blue glazing the walls. She loved the color blue, particularly this cobalt-blue glass one found on the Amalfi coast, and could imagine beautiful jewelry made from the same blue glass, round beads and square knots mixed with gold and shells and bits of wood and other things that caught her fancy.

Her fingers suddenly itched to pick up a pencil and sketch some designs, not the extravagant gold cuffs and collars from her Amalfi collection, but something lighter, simpler. These pieces would be more affordable, perhaps a little bit of a splurge for younger girls, but within reach if they'd saved their pennies. Morgan could imagine the trendy jet-setters buying up strands of different colors and textures and pairing them with easy bracelets, perfect to wear to dinner, or out shopping on a weekend, or on a beach in Greece.

"What are you thinking about?" Drakon asked from the doorway.

Startled, she gazed blankly at him, having forgotten for a moment where she was. "Jewelry," she said, feeling as if she'd been caught doing something naughty. "Why?"

"You were smiling a little…as if you were daydreaming."

"I suppose I was. It helps me to imagine designing things. Makes the loss of my company less painful."

"You'll have another store again."

"It'd be fiscally irresponsible. My last collection nearly bankrupted me."

One of the kitchen staff appeared with an espresso for Drakon and handed it to him. He nodded toward the table. "May I join you?"

"Of course you may, but I was just about to leave," she said.

"Then don't let me keep you," he answered.

His voice didn't change—it remained deep, smooth, even—but she saw something in his face, a shadow in his eyes, and she suddenly felt vile. Here he was, helping her, supporting her, extending himself emotionally and financially, and she couldn't even be bothered to sit with him while he had breakfast?

"But if you don't mind my company," she added quickly, "I'll have another coffee and stay."

There was another flicker in his eyes, this one harder to read, and after sitting down across from her, he rang the bell and ordered another coffee for her, along with his breakfast.

They talked about trivial things over breakfast like the weather and movies and books they'd read lately. Morgan was grateful their talk was light and impersonal. She was finding it hard to concentrate in the first place, never mind carry on a conversation. Drakon was so beautiful this morning with his dark hair still slightly damp from his shower and his jaw freshly shaven. The morning light gilded him, with the sun playing across his strong, handsome features, illuminating his broad brow, his straight Greek nose, his firm full mouth.

It was impossible to believe this gorgeous, gorgeous man had been her husband. She was mad to leave him. But then, living with him had made her insane.

Drakon's black brows tugged. "It's going to be all right. Rowan should be here in the next hour. We'll soon have information about your father."

"Thank you," she said quietly.

"Last night after you'd gone to bed I was thinking about everything you said yesterday—" He broke off, frowning. "Am I really such an ogre, Morgan? Why do you think I would judge you...and judge you so harshly?"

His gaze, so direct, so piercing, unnerved her. She smoothed the edge of the yellow square cloth where it met the blue underskirt. "Your corporation is worth billions of dollars and your work is vital to Greece and world's economy. I'm nothing. I do nothing. I add little value—"

"Life isn't just about drudgery. It is also about beauty, and you bring beauty into the world." The heat in his eyes reminded her of their courtship, where he'd watched her across ballrooms with that lazy, sensual gleam in his eyes, his expression one of pride and pleasure as well as possession. She'd felt powerful with his eyes on her. Beautiful and important.

"But I don't think important thoughts. I don't discuss relevant topics."

"Relevant to whom?"

"To you! I bore you—"

"Where do you get these ideas from?"

"From you." She swallowed hard and forced herself to hold

his gaze even though it was so incredibly uncomfortable. "I annoyed you when we lived together. And I don't blame you. I know you find people like me irritating."

His black eyebrows pulled and his jaw jutted. "People like you? What does that mean?"

She shrugged uneasily, wishing she hadn't said anything. She hadn't meant anything by it.

No, not true. She had. She still remembered how he had shut down her attempts at conversation once their honeymoon had ended and they'd returned to Greece, remembered their silent lonely evenings in their sprawling modern white marble villa. Drakon would arrive home from work and they'd sit in the dining room, but it'd been a silent meal, with Drakon often reviewing papers or something on his tablet and then afterward he'd retreat to a chair in the living room and continue reading until bed. Once in the bedroom, things changed. Behind the closed door, he'd want hot, erotic sex, and for twenty minutes or sixty, or even longer depending on the night, he'd be alive, and sensual, utterly engrossed with her body and pleasure, and then when it was over, he'd fall asleep, and in the morning when she woke, he'd be gone, back to his office.

"People like me who don't read the business section of the newspaper. People like me who don't care passionately about politics. People like me who don't make money but spend it." She lifted her chin and smiled at him, a hard dazzling smile to hide how much those memories still hurt. "People who can only talk about fashion and shopping and which restaurants are considered trendy."

He tapped his finger on the table. "I do not understand the way you say, 'people like you.' I've never met anyone like you. For me, there is you, and only you."

She leaned forward, her gaze locking with his. "Why did you marry me, Drakon?"

"Because I wanted you. You were made for me. Meant for me."

"What did you like about me?"

"Everything."

"That's not true."

"It is true. I loved your beauty, your intelligence, your warmth, your passion, your smile, your laugh."

She noticed he said *loved,* past tense, and it hurt, a hot lance of pain straight through her heart. Perhaps it was merely a slip, or possibly, a grammatical error, but both were unlikely. Drakon didn't make mistakes.

"But you know that," he added brusquely.

"No," she said equally roughly, "I didn't know that. I had no idea why you cared about me, or if you even cared for me—"

"How can you say such a thing?"

"Because you never talked to me!" she cried. "After our honeymoon ended, you disappeared."

"I merely went back to work, Morgan."

"Yes, but you worked twelve- and fourteen-hour days, which would have been fine, but when you came home, you were utterly silent."

"I was tired. I work long days."

"And I was home alone all day with servants who didn't speak English."

"You promised me you were going to learn Greek."

"I did, I took lessons at the language school in Athens, but when you came home at night, you were irritated by my attempts to speak Greek, insisting we converse in English—" She compressed her lips, feeling the resentment and frustration bubble up. "And then when I tried to make friends, I kept bumping into your old girlfriends and lovers. Athens is full of them. How many women have you been with, Drakon?"

"You make it sound like you met dozens of exes, but you bumped into just three."

"You're right, just three, and in hindsight, they were actually much nicer than the Greek socialites I met who were furious that I'd stolen Greece's most eligible bachelor from under their noses." Morgan's eyes sparkled dangerously. "How could I, a trashy American, take one of Greece's national treasures?"

"It wasn't that bad."

"It was that bad! Everybody hated me before I even arrived!" She leaned across the table. "You should have warned me, Drakon. Prepared me for my new married life."

"I didn't know...hadn't realized...that some of the ladies would be so catty, but I always came home to you every night."

"No, I didn't have you. That was the problem."

"What do you mean?"

Morgan laughed coolly. "You came home to dinner, a bed and sex, but you didn't come home to me, because if you had, you would have talked to me, and tried to speak Greek to me, and you would have helped me meet people, instead of getting annoyed with me for caring what Greek women thought of me."

He swore violently and got up from the table, pacing the floor once before turning to look at her. "I can't believe this is why you left me. I can't believe you'd walk out on me, and our marriage, because I'm not one for conversation. I've never been a big talker, but coming home to you was my favorite part of the day. It's what I looked forward to all day long, from the moment I left for my office."

She swallowed around the lump filling her throat. "And yet when Bronwyn called you at home, you'd talk to her for hours."

"Not for hours."

"For thirty minutes at a time. Over and over every night."

"We had business to discuss."

"And could nothing wait until the morning? Was everything really a crisis? Or could she just not make a decision without you?"

"Is that why you left me? Because of Bronwyn?"

Yes, she wanted to say. Yes, yes, yes. But in her heart she knew Bronwyn Harper was only part of the issue. Drakon's close relationship with his Australian vice president only emphasized how lonely and empty Morgan felt with him. "Bronwyn's constant presence in our lives didn't help matters. Every time I turned around, she was there, and you did talk to her, whereas you didn't talk to me."

The fight abruptly left her, and once her anger deserted her, she was exhausted and flattened, depressed by a specter of what they had been, and the illusion of what she'd hoped they'd be. "But it's a moot point now. It doesn't matter—" She broke off. "My God! You're doing it now. Rolling your eyes! Looking utterly bored and annoyed."

"I'm frustrated, Morgan, and yes, I do find this entire conversation annoying because you're putting words in my mouth, telling me how I felt, and I'm telling you I didn't feel that way when we were married."

"Don't you remember telling me repeatedly that you had people—*women*—talking at you at work, and that you didn't need me talking at you at home? Don't you remember telling me, you preferred silence—"

"I remember telling you that *once,* because I did come home one day needing quiet, and I wanted you to know it wasn't personal, and that I wasn't upset with you, that it had simply been a long day with a lot of people talking at me." He walked toward her, his gaze hard, his expression forbidding. "And instead of you being understanding, you went into hysterics, crying and raging—"

"I wasn't hysterical."

"You had no right to be upset, though." He was standing before her now. "I'd just lost two members of my crew from a hijacked ship and I'd had to tell the families that their loved ones were gone and it was a bad, bad day. A truly awful day."

"Then tell me next time that something horrific has happened, and I'll understand, but don't just disappear into your office and give me the silent treatment."

"I shouldn't have to talk if I don't want to talk."

"I was your wife. If something important happens in your world, I'd like to know."

"It's not as if you could do anything."

"But I could care, Drakon, and I would at least know what's happening in your life and I could grieve for the families of your crew, too, because I would have grieved, and I would have wanted to comfort you—"

"I don't need comforting."

"Clearly." Hot, sharp emotions rushed through her, one after the other, and she gave her head a fierce, decisive shake. "Just as you clearly didn't need me, either, because you don't need anything, Drakon Xanthis. You're perfect and complete just the way you are!"

She brushed past him and walked out, not quickly, or tearfully, but resolutely, reassured all over again that she had done the right thing in leaving him. He really didn't want a wife, or a partner, someone that was equal and valuable. He only wanted a woman for physical release. In his mind, that was all a woman was good for, and thank God she'd left when she had or he would have destroyed her completely.

Drakon caught up with her in the narrow stairway at the back of the villa. It had once been the staircase for the servants and was quite simple with plain plaster walls and steep, small stairs, but it saved Morgan traversing the long hallway.

He clasped her elbow, stopping her midstep. "You are so very good at running away, Morgan."

She shook him off and turned to face him. He was standing two steps down but that still put them on eye level and she stared into his eyes, so very full of anger and pain. "And you are so good at shutting people out!"

"I don't need to report to you, Morgan. You are my wife, not my colleague."

"And funny enough, I would rather have been your colleague than your wife. At least you would have talked to me!"

"But then there would have been no lovemaking."

"Perhaps it will surprise you to know that I'm actually far more interested in what's in your brain than what's in your trousers." She saw his incredulous expression and drew a ragged breath, horrified all over again that their entire relationship had been based on sex and chemistry. Horrified that she'd married a man who only wanted her for her body. "It's true. Lovemaking is empty without friendship, and we had no friendship, Drakon. We just had sex—"

"Not this again!"

"Yes, this again."

"You're being absurd."

"Thank God we'll both soon be free so we can find someone that suits us both better. You can go get another pretty girl and give her an orgasm once or twice a day and feel like a real man, and I'll find a man who has warmth and compassion, a man who cares about what I think and feel, a man who wants to know *me,* and not just my body!"

He came up one step, and then another until they were on the same narrow stair, crowding her so that her back was against the plaster of the stairwell, and his big body was almost touching hers.

A dangerous light shone in his eyes, making her blood hum in her veins and her nerves dance. "Is that all I'm interested in? Your body?" he growled, a small muscle popping in his jaw.

She stared at his jaw, fascinated by that telling display of temper. He was angry and this was all so new...his temper and emotion. She'd always thought of him as supremely controlled but his tension was palpable now. He practically seethed with frustration and it made her skin tingle, particularly her lips, which suddenly felt unbearably sensitive. "Apparently so."

He stepped even closer, his eyes glittering down at her. "I wish I'd known that before I married you. It would have saved me half a billion dollars, never mind years of trouble."

"We all make mistakes," she taunted, deliberately provoking him, but unable to help herself. Drakon Xanthis's famous icy control was cracking and she wondered what would happen when it shattered completely. "Best thing you can do now is forgive yourself for making such a dreadful mistake and move forward."

Fire flashed in his eyes and he leaned in, closing the gap between them so that his broad chest just grazed the swell of her breasts and she could feel the tantalizing heat of his hips so close to hers.

"Such an interesting way to view things," he said, his head dropping, his voice deepening. "With you as my mistake."

His lips were so close now and her lower back tingled and her belly tightened, and desire coursed through her veins, making her ache everywhere.

She could feel his need, feel the desire and her mouth dried, her heart hammering harder. He was going to kiss her. And she wanted the kiss, craved his kiss, even as a little voice of reason inside her head sounded the alarm....

Stop. Wait. Think.

She had to remember...remember the past...remember what had happened last time...this wasn't just a kiss, but an inferno. If she gave in to this kiss, it'd be all over. Drakon was so dangerous for her. He did something to her. He, like his name, Drakon, Greek for dragon, was powerful and potent and destructive.

But he was also beautiful and physical and sensual and

he made her *feel.* My God, he made her feel and she wanted that intensity now. Wanted him now.

"My beautiful, expensive mistake," he murmured, his lips brushing across the shell of her ear, making her breath catch in her throat and sending hot darts of delicious sensation throughout her body, making her aware of every sensitive spot.

"Next time, don't marry the girl," she said, trying to sound brazen and cavalier, but failing miserably as just then he pushed his thigh between her legs. The heat of his hard body scalded her, and the unexpected pressure and pleasure was so intense she gasped, making her head spin.

"Would you have been happier just being my mistress?" he asked, his tongue tracing the curve of her ear even as his muscular thigh pressed up, his knee against her core, teasing her senses, making her shiver with need.

She was wet and hot, too hot, and her skin felt too tight. She wanted relief, needed relief, and it didn't help that she couldn't catch her breath. She was breathing shallowly, her chest rising and falling while her mouth dried.

"Would you have been able to let go more? Enjoyed the sex without guilt?" he added, biting her tender earlobe, his teeth sharp, even as he wedged his thigh deeper between her knees, parting her thighs wider so that she felt like a butterfly pinned against the wall.

"There was no guilt," she choked, eyes closing as he worked his thigh against her in a slow maddening circle. He was so warm and she was so wet and she knew it was wrong, but she wanted more, not less.

His teeth scraped across that hollow beneath her ear and she shuddered against him, thinking he remembered how sensitive she was, how her body responded to every little touch and bite and caress.

"Liar." He leaned in closer, his knee grinding and his hips pressing down against her hips, making her pelvis feel hot and yet hollow, and the muscles inside her womb clench. "You liked it hot. You liked it when I made you fall apart."

And it was true, she thought, her body so tight and hot and aching that she arched against him, absolutely wanton. There was no satisfaction like this, though, and she wanted satisfaction. Wanted him. Wanted him here and now. Wanted him to lift her tunic and expose her breasts and knead and roll the tight, aching nipples between his fingers. He'd made her come that way before, just by playing with her nipples, and he'd watched her face as she came, watched every flicker of emotion that crossed her face as he broke her control....

If only he'd peel her clothes off now, if only she could feel his skin on her skin, feel him in her, needing the heat and fullness of him inside her, craving the pleasure of being taken, owned, possessed—

Morgan's eyes flew open.

Owned?

Owned? My God. She *was* insane.

Visions of her months at McLean Hospital filled her head and it dragged her abruptly back to reality. She had to be smart. Couldn't destroy herself again. Never wanted to go back to McLean Hospital again.

The very memory of McLean was enough for her to put her hands on his chest and push him back, and she pushed hard, but he didn't budge and all she felt was the warm dense plane of muscle that banded his ribs, and the softness of his cashmere sweater over the dense carved muscle.

"Get off," she panted, pushing harder, putting all of her weight into the shove but Drakon was solid, immoveable. "I'm not a toy, Drakon, not here for your amusement."

His hand snaked into her hair, twisting the dark length around his fist, holding her face up to his. "Good, because I'm not amused."

"No, you're just aroused," she answered coldly, furious

with herself for responding to him with such abandon. So typical. So pathetic. No wonder her family had locked her up.

He caught one of her hands and dragged it down his body and between their hips to cup his erection. "Yes," he drawled, amber gaze burning, "so I am."

She inhaled sharply, her fingers curving around him, clasping his thick shaft as if measuring the hard length, and it was a terrible seductive pleasure, touching him like this. She remembered how he felt inside her—hot, heavy—and how the satin heat of his body would stretch her, stroke her, hitting nerve endings she hadn't even known she had.

Curiosity and desire warred with her sense of self-preservation, before overriding her common sense.

Morgan palmed the length of him, slowly, firmly running her hand down his shaft and then, as if unable to stop herself, back up again to cup the thick, rounded head. She'd never thought a man's body was beautiful before she'd met Drakon, but she loved every muscle and shadow of his body, loved the lines and the planes and the way his cock hung heavy between his muscular legs. He was such a powerfully built man, and yet the skin on his shaft was so smooth and sensitive, like silk, and the contradiction between his great, hard body and that delicate skin fascinated her.

But then he fascinated her. No, it was more than that, more than fascination. It was an obsession. She needed him so much she found it virtually impossible to live without him.

"You want me," he said. "You want me to peel your trousers and knickers off and take you here, on these steps, don't you?"

Fire surged through her veins, fire and hunger and shame. Because yes, she did want him and her orgasms were the most intense when he pushed it to the edge, making every touch into something dangerous and erotic. "You do like to dominate," she answered breathlessly.

He tugged on her hair, and it hurt a little, just as he'd intended, making her nipples harden into tight, aching buds even as she stiffened against him, her body rippling with need.

"And you do like to be dominated," he rasped in her ear.

CHAPTER SIX

SHE SHOVED AWAY from him and this time he let her go and Morgan ran the rest of the way up the stairs, racing back to her room, his voice echoing in her head. *And you like to be dominated... .*

Morgan barely made it to her bed before her legs gave out, the mocking words making her absolutely heartsick, because he wasn't completely wrong. Part of her did like it. It was sexy...hot...exciting.

But she shouldn't like it. It wasn't politically correct. She couldn't imagine her mother approving. Not that she wanted to think about her mother and sex at the same time...or even about sex in general since she wasn't going to be having sex anytime soon and God help her, she wanted to.

She wanted to be ravished. Stripped. Tied up. Taken. Tasted. Devoured—

Oh, God, she was mad, she was. What sane woman wanted to be ravished? What kind of woman ached to be tied up and taken? Tasted?

What was wrong with her?

Before Drakon she'd never had these thoughts. She'd never imagined that sex could make one feel absolutely wild. She'd never dreamed that desire could be an uncontrollable fire that made one lose all perspective...as well as one's reason....

But desire was an inferno, and she felt absolutely consumed by need now. Lying facedown on her bed, her body ached with need. Her skin burned, her senses swam. Every muscle in her body felt taut and every nerve ending far too tight. She wanted relief, craved release, and the fact that she couldn't have it made the aching emptiness worse.

Morgan buried her face in a pillow and knotted her fists and screamed. And screamed some more.

She wanted him. She wanted him, wanted him, wanted him and he could give her what she wanted, too. He'd do it. He'd do anything she wanted and yet it was wrong. They weren't together, they hadn't been together in years, and she couldn't use him to scratch an itch...no matter how powerful the itch.

And yet, oh, God, her body ached and throbbed and she felt wild...hot and tense and so very raw.

Dammit. Damn him. Damn that kiss in the stairwell. Damn this terrible incredible unforgettable chemistry.

It wasn't right to want him this much still. Wasn't fair to still feel so much, either, especially when she knew how bad he was for her, how very destructive. She couldn't blame him entirely. The doctors said the problem was hers...that she didn't have proper boundaries. She didn't have a clear or strong sense of self and the only way she'd achieve a strong, mature sense of self was by leaving Drakon....

As if it were that easy...

Just leave him. Forget him. Forget he ever existed...

And now he was downstairs, so intense and real, so physical, so sensual, so fiercely beautiful.

Morgan beat the bed with her fist, maddened by the futility of her desire. Blood drummed in her veins, need coiled tightly, hotly in her belly, and her entire body ached with emptiness. How could emptiness throb and pulse? How could emptiness burn? But it did. And she felt wild and furious and frustrated beyond reason.

If only she could go to him, and beg for him to help her, beg him to give her release. Beg for pleasure.

She'd happily crawl for him, crawl to him, if it meant that he could tame the beast inside her...that voracious hunger that made her feel too wild, too frantic, too much.

Drakon stood just inside the doorway of Morgan's suite and watched her beat her fist against the bed, her dark hair gleaming, her tunic riding high on her thighs, the soft fabric clinging to the firm, rounded curves of her hips and butt.

She had a gorgeous butt, and it made him want to spank her, restrain her, knowing it'd arouse her, make things hotter, make her wet and anxious and hungry for him.

And then he'd make love to her.

With his mouth, his tongue, his teeth, his hands, his cock. He loved the softness of her skin and the scent of her, the way she blushed, the way her tongue traveled across the bow of her upper lip and the way she'd squirm beneath him, her slim body arching, her hips grinding up to meet his, her legs opening for him.

"Undress," he said, his voice pitched so low it sounded like a growl.

Morgan swiftly sat up, eyes enormous in her face, cheeks flushed.

"Do it," he said, folding his arms across his chest.

Her lips parted in silent protest and yet he knew she was tempted, seriously tempted, because she wanted the same thing he did—excitement, pleasure, release.

"And what?" she whispered, her tongue darting to her lower lip, moistening it.

He was already hard. Now he wanted to explode. "And let me look at you. I want to see you, my beautiful wife."

"I'm not your wife."

"Oh, you are my wife. And have been my wife and will be my wife until the day the divorce is granted. Then...you'll be someone else's woman, but until then, you are mine. And

you know you are. That is why you came here to me, wanting my help. You knew I'd refuse you nothing."

He saw the flicker in her eyes, that recognition of truth.
"Just as you know I've never refused you anything," she
whispered, her voice unsteady.

No, she hadn't, he thought, his shaft growing even harder,
making him hotter, remembering how she always responded
to him.

He'd known plenty of women who liked hot sex, but he'd
never been with anyone as passionate as Morgan. She wasn't
comfortable with her passionate nature, though, and during
their six months together she'd struggled with the concept
of physical pleasure, and resisted giving in to her sensual
side, viewing it as a weakness, or something shameful, instead of an intimacy that brought them closer together...
binding, bonding, making them one. "But I've never forced
you, Morgan—"

"Not forced, no, but you have pushed me, pushed me beyond what I was comfortable doing."

"Isn't that exciting, though? To try new things...explore
new things...to know and then go outside your comfort zone?"

Another flicker of emotion passed over her lovely face.
She had such fine, elegant features, as well as that famous
Copeland reserve, a trait shared by her equally glamorous
sisters. The reserve came from the way they'd been raised...
from birth they'd been privileged, and had enjoyed a luxurious lifestyle of private schools, private jets, private islands.
Their money attracted attention, and men, lots and lots of
men, and by the time the four Copeland girls had become
women, they knew they were special. Unique. They believed
they deserved better.

Drakon had been drawn to Morgan's beauty, but also her
reserve. He'd viewed it as a challenge to break through her
cool, haughty exterior to discover the warm woman under-
neath.

And once he'd touched her, she'd been more than warm. She'd burned as if consumed by a fever and during their honeymoon, those four weeks here at Villa Angelica, he'd enjoyed discovering the depths of her passion and exploring her desires, her fears and her limits.

"But everything with you was outside my comfort zone," she said, trying to hide the quiver of her lower lip. "Everything was overwhelming."

She'd said this once before to him, during the last week of their honeymoon after an erotic afternoon on a private island, and he'd been startled that her memory of lovemaking on the pristine ivory beach had been so different from what he'd felt. Returning to his yacht, which had been anchored off the island while they picnicked on the beach, he had never felt closer to her, or more committed, and he'd been shocked when she accused him of taking advantage of her. Shocked and sickened.

He was Greek—a man of surprisingly simple tastes. He valued his family, his friends and his culture, which included good food, good drink and great sex. He wouldn't apologize for enjoying sex, either, or enjoying his wife's beautiful body. What did she expect him to do? Pretend he didn't like sex? Act as though he didn't find pleasure in her warmth and softness?

Back in Athens after the honeymoon, Drakon had tried to be the husband she wanted. He stopped reaching for her quite as often, and then when he did reach for her, he changed the way he touched her, holding back to keep from overwhelming her. He knew she didn't like it when he expressed hunger, or focused too much on her pleasure, and so instead of just being with her, and enjoying her, he practiced control and distance, hoping that a less passionate husband would be more to her liking.

Instead she'd left.

And just remembering how he'd turned himself inside

out trying to please her, trying to give her what she wanted, made him angry all over again now.

He'd hated second-guessing himself back then, hated not being able to please her, hated failing as a husband.

His gaze swept over her, slowly, critically, examining her as if he owned her, and he did...at least for a few more weeks.

"Undress," he said roughly, feeling raw and so very carnal, and liking it. Enjoying it. "I want to see my wife. It doesn't seem like too much to ask for, not after giving you seven million dollars."

One of her eyebrows lifted. "At least you didn't mention the four hundred million."

"That was to your father, not to you."

"I wonder what he had to do for four hundred million."

"You think I should have asked for some sexual favors, do you?"

"You like sex a lot."

"I liked it with you a lot." He suddenly reached down, palmed his erection through his trousers, and he saw her gaze settle on his shaft, measuring the length and size.

Dark pink color stormed her cheeks and she licked her lower lip, once and again, before finding her voice. "That's obscene," she whispered.

"You did it a moment ago."

"You made me."

"You liked it. But you'll tell me you didn't. You'll tell me sex is disgusting. You'll tell me I'm disgusting, but if I touched you now, my woman, you'd be dripping wet—"

"Disgusting."

"And I'd open you and lick you and taste you and make you come." His head cocked and he shoved his hands in his trouser pockets. "When is the last time you came? How long has it been since you had an orgasm? A day? A week? A month?"

"It's none of your business."

"I did it in the shower yesterday, before you arrived. Stroked myself as I thought about you, picturing your breasts and your pale thighs and how much I enjoy being between them."

"Is there any point to this, Drakon? Or do you just wish to humiliate me?"

"Humiliate you, how? By telling you how much I want you, even now, even after you walked out on me?"

"But you don't want me, you just want to have sex with me."

"That's right. You don't believe you're attached to your body, or that your body is part of you. Instead it's a separate entity, which makes me think of a headless chicken—"

"Don't be rude."

"Then stop jumping to conclusions. Just because I like your body, doesn't mean I don't appreciate the rest of you."

"Humph!"

His eyebrows shot up, his expression mocking. "Is that the best you can do?"

She crossed her arms over her chest, her chin jerking up. "I get nowhere arguing with you."

"Very wise. Much better to just dispense with the clothing and let me have what I want." He paused, and his gaze moved slowly, suggestively over her. "And what I know you want, too. Not that you'll admit it."

Her chin lifted another notch. "And what do I want?"

"Satisfying sex without pushing the limits too far."

Dark pink color stormed her cheeks. "Without pushing the limits at all."

The corners of his mouth curled. So she did want sex. Just nice-girl sex…sweet, safe missionary-position sex. His cock throbbed at the thought. He'd like some sweet, safe-missionary sex as well. "I'll see what I can do. But first, I'd like to see you. But I'm getting bored by all the discussion. Either we're going to do this, or we're not—"

"Your shirt first."

"Excuse me?"

"You want to do this? Then we'll do this. But you're not the boss and I'm not taking orders." Her tone was defiant and her eyes flashed and she'd never been angry before when they'd played these games. She'd been shy and nervous, but also eager to please. She wasn't eager to please now. "You don't get to have all the power anymore."

"No?"

"No. I'm not your servant or slave—"

"Which is good, since I don't make love with my servants, and I don't have slaves."

"The point is, you might be able to bark orders at Bronwyn, but not at me."

"I had no idea you were so hung up on Bronwyn," he drawled, liking this new feisty Morgan. She was a very different woman from the one he'd married and that intrigued him.

"I wasn't hung up on her. You were."

"Is that how it was?"

"Yes."

"So are we going to talk about Bronwyn, or are we going to have sweet, safe missionary-position sex?"

Her lips compressed primly. "You're horrible. You know that, don't you?"

"Horribly good, and horribly hard, and horribly impatient. Now, are we, or aren't we?" he asked, sauntering toward her, relaxed, easy, his arms loose at his sides. But it was a deceptive ease, and they both knew it as the temperature in the luxurious bedroom seemed to soar and the air sparked with heat and need, the tension between them thick and hot and electric.

Closing the gap between them, Drakon could feel Morgan tense, her hands squeezing in convulsive fists, even as her eyes widened and her lips parted with each quick shallow breath.

"You're trembling," he said, "but there's no need for that. I won't eat you. Not unless you want me to."

"Drakon." Her voice sounded strangled and her cheeks were crimson, making her blue eyes darken and shimmer like the sapphire sea beyond the window.

"I hope you'll want me to. I love how you taste, and how soft you are in my mouth...so sweet. But is that too risky for you? Pushing the limits too much?"

"You love to torment me."

"Yes, I do," he agreed, circling her slowly, enjoying just looking at her, and watching the color come and go in her exquisite porcelain complexion, and listening to her soft desperate gasps of air. "But this is nothing, Morgan. I haven't even gotten started." He stopped in front of her, gazed down at her, thinking she looked very young and very uncertain and very shy, much like his virgin bride. "Now tell me, what should I do to you first?"

Morgan's heart was pounding so fast she couldn't catch her breath, and she opened her mouth, lips parting, to gulp in shallow gasps of air. She felt as if she were balancing on the edge of a volcano while little voices inside her head demanded she throw herself in.

She needed to leave, to escape the villa, to summon the helicopter and fly far, far away. Remaining here with Drakon was stupid and destructive. She might as well fling herself into that volcano...the outcome would be the same.

And yet, wasn't she already there, in the fiery pit? Because molten lava seemed to be seeping through her veins, melting her bones and muscles into mindless puddles of want and need.

She actually felt sick with need right now. But could she do this...go through with this...knowing it would be just sex, not love? Knowing Drakon wanted her body but not her heart?

"Are you crying?" he asked, his voice dropping, deepening with concern, as his hands wrapped around her arms, holding her up.

She shook her head, unable to look him in the eye.

"What's wrong?" he asked.

She swallowed hard, tried to speak, but no sound would come out. Not when her throat ached and her heart was still thundering in her chest.

He reached up to smooth a dark tendril of hair back from her face. "Have I frightened you?" His deep voice was suddenly gentle, almost painfully tender.

Hot tears scalded the back of her eyes. She bit hard into her lower lip so that it wouldn't quiver.

"I would never hurt you, Morgan," he murmured, drawing her against him, holding her in his arms, holding her securely against his chest.

She closed her eyes as the heat of his body seeped into her hands, warming her. He felt good. Too good. It was so confusing. This was confusing.

She didn't push him away, and yet she couldn't relax, waiting for the moment he'd let her go. But she didn't want him to let her go. She wanted him closer. Wanted to press her face to his chest and breathe him in. She could smell a hint of his spicy fragrance and loved that fragrance—his own scent, formulated just for him—and what it did to his skin. He smelled like heaven. Delicious and warm and good and intoxicating. He smelled like everything she wanted. He smelled like home. He *was* home. He was everything to her, but wasn't that the problem? With him, she lost herself. With him, she lost her mind.

With a strangled cry, Morgan slid a hand up across his chest, to push him back, and just like before, once she touched him, she couldn't take her hand away. She stroked across the hard plane of muscle of his chest, learning again the shape of his body and how the dense smooth pectoral muscle curved and sloped beneath her palm. God, he was beautiful. And without his shirt, his skin would feel so good against hers. She loved the way his bare chest felt against her bare breasts, loved the friction and the heat and the delicious, addictive energy—

"Can't do this," she choked, shaking her head. "We can't, we can't."

"Ssshh," he murmured, cupping her face, his thumbs stroking lightly over her cheekbones, sweeping from the curve of the bone to her earlobes. "Nothing bad will happen—"

"Everything bad will happen," she protested, shivering with pleasure from the caress. She loved the way he touched her. He made her feel beautiful, inside and out, and she struggled to remember what bad things would happen if he touched her....

"You are so beautiful," he murmured, hands slipping from her face to tangle in her hair.

"And mad, Drakon, certifiably insane—"

"That's okay."

"Drakon, I'm serious!"

"I am, too." His head dipped lower and his lips brushed hers, lightly, slowly, and she shuddered, pressed closer, a stinging sensation behind her eyes. One kiss...could it be so bad? One kiss...surely she could be forgiven that?

His lips found hers again and the kiss was surprisingly gentle, the pressure of his mouth just enough to tease her, send shivers of desire racing up and down her spine. This was all so impossible. They couldn't do this, couldn't give in to this, it's all they had and while the chemistry was intense, chemistry wasn't enough. Sex wasn't enough. She needed more. She needed a relationship, love, intimacy, commitment, but right now, she also needed this.

She'd missed him so much. Missed his skin and his scent, his warmth and his strength, and her defenses caved as his hands framed her face, and he held her face to his, deepening the kiss, drinking her in.

She could feel him and smell him and taste him now and she was lost. Nothing felt better than this. Nothing felt better than him. He wasn't just her husband, he was home and happiness—

No. No, no, no. Couldn't think that way, couldn't lose sight of reality. He wasn't home or happiness. And he'd finally agreed to let her go. After five years of wanting out, and she *did* want out, she was free.

And yet when his tongue stroked the seam of her lips, she arched and gasped, opening her mouth to him. Drakon deepened the kiss, his tongue flicking the inside of her lip, making every little nerve dance. One of his hands slid from the back of her head, down over her shoulders to her waist before settling in the small of her spine, urging her closer, shaping her against his powerful body.

She shuddered with pleasure as his tongue filled her mouth and the fingers of his hand splayed wider on her back, making her lower belly throb, ache, just like her thighs ached.

Every thrust of his tongue shot another bright arc of sensation through her, sensation that surged to the tips of her breasts, tightening them into hard, sensitive peaks, and then deep into her belly and even deeper to her innermost place, and yet it wasn't enough, not even close. Morgan dug her nails into his shoulders, pressing her breasts to his chest, practically grinding herself against his hips to feel the ridge of his erection rub against her sensitive spot at the junction of her thighs and the heat of his palm against her lower back.

It was still so electric between them, still fierce and wild, and she felt overwhelmed by desire, overwhelmed by the memory of such dizzying, maddening pleasure and the knowledge that he was here, and there could be more. And right now, she wanted more. She literally ached for him and could feel her body soften and warm for him, her body also clearly remembering that nothing in the world felt better than him in her. Him with her.

And then his hand was slipping slowly across the curve of her hip, to cup the roundness of her butt, and she nearly popped out of her skin. "Drakon," she groaned against his mouth, feeling as if he were spreading fire through her, fire and such fierce, consuming need.

She trembled as he stroked the length of her, from her hip to her breast and down again. His hands were everywhere now, pinching a nipple, stroking the cleft of her buttocks, shaping her thighs. She wanted his hand between her thighs, wanted him to touch her, fill her, wanted him more than she'd wanted anything—

Wait.

Wait.

She struggled to focus, clear her head, which was impossible with Drakon's amazing hands on her body and his mouth taking hers, promising her endless pleasure.

She had to move back, away, had to, now.

But then his hands were up, under her tunic, his skin so warm against hers, and when he unhooked her bra to cup her breasts, his thumbs grazing her tight, swollen nipples, she gave up resisting, gave up thinking and gave in to him.

He stripped off her clothes while kissing her, his hands never leaving her body as the clothes fell away, giving her no time to panic or reconsider.

Once naked, he carried her to the bed, and set her on her back in the middle of the enormous bed. The room's windows and doors were open and the sunlight spilled across the floor, splashing on the walls while the heady sweet scent of wisteria filled the room.

Morgan watched Drakon's face as he moved over her, his hard, powerful body warm, his skin a burnished gold, his strong features taut with passion. But it was his eyes that once again captivated her, and the burning intensity of his gaze. When he looked at her he made her feel extraordinary...desirable...rare...impossibly valuable. She knew he didn't feel that way about her, not anymore, but with him stretched out over her, his skin covering her, warming her, it didn't seem to matter.

She lifted her face to his, and his mouth met hers in a blistering kiss that melted everything within her. There was nothing she wouldn't give him. And as he settled his weight between her thighs, his hips pressing down against hers, she shivered with pleasure.

He was resting his weight on his forearms, but she wanted more pressure, not less, and Morgan arched up, pressing her breasts to his bare chest, loving the friction of his nipples on hers even as she opened her thighs wider, letting him settle deeper into her.

"I want you," she whispered against his mouth, her arms circling his shoulders, her hands sliding into his thick hair, fingers curling into the crisp strands at his nape. He felt good and smelled good and in this moment, everything was right in the world...at least, everything was right in her world. "I want you in me. I need you in me."

"It's been a long time."

"Too long," she said, lifting her hips, grinding up against him, not wanting any more foreplay, not wanting anything but him, and his body meshed deeply with hers.

"Patience," he answered, kissing the corner of her mouth and the line of her jaw, smoothing her hair back from her face. "There's no need to rush—"

But there was. She didn't want to wait, had enough teasing and words and thinking, had enough of everything but him. And right now she just wanted him. She reached between them, caught his hard shaft and gripped it firmly, the way she knew he liked it, and rubbed his head up and down her, the warm, rigid shaft sliding across her damp opening, making him slick, and then bringing the silken head up to her sensitive nub, drawing moisture up over her clit.

She heard him groan deep in his throat, a hoarse, guttural sound of pleasure, and it gave her a perverse thrill, knowing she could make Drakon feel something so strong that he'd groan aloud.

His hands stroked the outsides of her thighs and then down the inside and she shifted her hips, positioning him at her wet, slick core. "Do you want me?" she whispered, her lips at his ear.

"Yes," he groaned, his voice so low that it rumbled through her. "Yes, always."

And then he took control, lowering his weight, forearms pressed to the bed, and kissed her, deeply, his tongue plunging into her mouth even as he entered her body, thrusting all the way until they were one, and for a nearly a minute he remained still, kissing her, filling her, until she felt him swell inside her, stretching her, throbbing inside her, making her throb, too. Her pulse raced and her body tingled and burned, her inner muscles clenching and rippling with exquisite sensation. He was big and hard and warm and she could come like this, with her body gripping him, holding him, and Drakon knew it, knew how just being inside her could shatter her.

"Not yet," she gasped, hands stroking over his broad shoulders and down the smooth, hard, warm planes of his back, savoring the curve and hollow of every thick, sinewy muscle. Men were so beautiful compared to women, and no man was more beautiful than Drakon. "Don't let me come, not yet. I want more. I want everything."

And maybe this was just the plain old missionary position, but it felt amazing, felt hot and fierce and intense and emotional and physical and everything that was good. Sex like this was mind-blowingly good, especially with Drakon taking his time, thrusting into her in long smooth strokes that hit all the right places, that made her feel all the right things. Morgan wished it could last forever, but she was already responding, the muscles inside her womb were coiling tighter and tighter, bringing her ever closer to that point of no return. Morgan's head spun with the exquisite sensation, the tension so consuming that it was difficult to know in that moment if it was pleasure or pain, and then with one more deep thrust, Drakon sent her over the edge and her senses exploded, her body rippling and shuddering beneath his.

Drakon came while she was still climaxing and he ground out her name as he buried himself deeply within her. She could feel him come, feel the heat and liquid of him surging within her, and it hit her—they hadn't used a condom. On their honeymoon they had never used protection. Drakon wanted children and she wanted to please him and so they had never used birth control, but this was different. They were divorcing. She'd soon be single. There was absolutely no way she could cope with getting pregnant now.

"What have we done?" she cried, struggling to push him off of her. "What did we do?"

Drakon shifted his weight and allowed her to roll away from him, even as a small muscle jumped in his jaw. "I think you know what we just did."

"We shouldn't have. It was wrong."

"Doesn't feel wrong to me," he said tersely, watching her slide to the edge of the bed and search for her tunic, or something to cover up with.

She grabbed Drakon's shirt, and slipped it over her arms into the sleeves and buttoned up the front. "Well, it was. We didn't use birth control, Drakon, and we shouldn't have even thought about sex without using a condom."

"But we never used a condom."

"Because we were newlyweds. We were hoping to have

children, we both wanted a big family, but it's different now. We're separated. Divorcing. A baby would be disastrous, absolutely the worst thing possible—"

"Actually, I can think of a few things worse than a baby," he interrupted, getting off the bed and reaching for his trousers. He stepped into one leg and then the other before zipping them closed. "Like famine. Disease. Pestilence. Or someone swindling billions of dollars—"

"Obviously I didn't mean that a baby was a tragedy," she retorted, crossing her arms over her chest to hide the fact that she was trembling. Just moments ago she'd been so relaxed, so happy, and now she felt absolutely shell-shocked. How was it possible to swing from bliss to hell in thirty seconds flat? But then, wasn't that how it had always been with them?

"No, I think you did," he countered. "It's always about you, and what's good for you—"

"That's not true."

"Absolutely true. You're so caught up in what you want and need that there is no room in this relationship for two people. There certainly was never room for me."

Her eyes widened. "You can't be serious, Drakon. You're the most controlling person I've ever met. You controlled everything in our marriage, including me—"

"Do I look like I'm in control?" he demanded tautly, dark color washing the strong, hard planes of his face.

He was breathing unsteadily, and her gaze swept over him, from his piercing gaze to the high color in his cheekbones to his firm full mouth, and she thought he looked incredible. Beautiful. Powerful. Her very own mythic Greek god. But that was the problem. He was too beautiful, too powerful. She had no perspective around him. Would throw herself in the path of danger just to be close to him.

Good God. How self-destructive was that?

Before she could speak, she heard the distinctive hum of a helicopter.

"Rowan," Drakon said, crossing to the balcony and stepping outside to watch the helicopter move across the sky. "He'll have news about your father."

"Then I'd better shower and dress."

CHAPTER SEVEN

MORGAN REFUSED TO think about what had just happened in her bed, unable to go there at all, and instead focused on taking a very fast shower before drying off and changing into a simple A-line dress in white linen with blue piping that Drakon had shipped over from the Athens house with the rest of the wardrobe.

In the steamy marble bathroom, she ran a brush through her long hair before drawing it back into a sleek ponytail and headed for her door, careful to keep her gaze averted from the bed's tousled sheets and duvet.

The maid would remake the bed while she was gone, and probably change the sheets, and Morgan was glad. She didn't want to remember or reflect on what had just changed there. It shouldn't have happened. It was a terrible mistake.

She took the stairs quickly, overwhelmed by emotion— worry and hope for her father, longing for Drakon, as well as regret. Now that they'd made love once, would he expect her to tumble back into bed later tonight?

And what if he didn't want to make love again? What if that was the last time? How would she feel?

In some ways that was the worst thought of all.

It wasn't the right way to end things. Couldn't be their last time. Their last time needed to be different. Needed more, not less. Needed more emotion, more time, more skin, more love...

Love.

She still loved Drakon, didn't she? Morgan's eyes stung, knowing she always would love him, too. Saying goodbye to him would rip her heart out. She only hoped it'd be less destructive than it had been the first time. Could only hope she'd remember the pain was just grief...that the pain would eventually, one day, subside.

But she wouldn't go there, either. Not yet. She was still here with him, still feeling so alive with him. Better to stay focused on the moment, and deal with the future when it came.

Reaching the bottom stair she discovered one of Drakon's staff was waiting for her. "Mrs. Xanthis, Mr. Xanthis is waiting for you in the terrace sunroom," the maid said.

Morgan thanked her and headed down the final flight of stairs to the lower level, the terrace level.

The sunroom ran the length of the villa and had formerly been a ballroom in the nineteenth century. The ballroom's original gilt ceiling, the six sets of double glass doors and the grand Venetian glass chandeliers remained, but the grand space was filled now with gorgeous rugs and comfortable furniture places and potted palms and miniature citrus trees. It was one of the lightest, brightest rooms in the villa and almost always smelled of citrus blossoms.

Entering the former ballroom, Morgan spotted Drakon and another man standing in the middle of the enormous room, talking in front of a grouping of couches and chairs.

They both turned and looked at her as she entered the room, but Morgan only had eyes for Drakon. Just looking at him made her insides flip, and her pulse leap.

She needed him, wanted him, loved him, far too much.

Her heart raced and her stomach hurt as she crossed the ballroom, her gaze drinking in Drakon, her footsteps muffled by the plush Persian rugs scattered across the marble floor.

He looked amazing...like Drakon, but not like Drakon

in that soft gray knit shirt that hugged his broad shoulders and lovingly molded to his muscular chest, outlining every hard, sinewy muscle with a pair of jeans. In America they called shirts like the one he was wearing Henleys. They'd been work shirts, worn by farmers and firemen and lumberjacks, not tycoons and millionaires and it boggled her mind that Drakon would wear such a casual shirt, although from the look of the fabric and the cut, it wasn't an inexpensive one—but it suited him.

He looked relaxed...and warm. So warm. So absolutely not cold, or controlled. And part of her suddenly wondered, if he had ever been cold, or if she'd just come to think of him that way as they grew apart in those last few months of their marriage?

Which led to another question—had he ever been that much in control, too? Or had she turned him into something he wasn't? Her imagination making him into an intimidating and controlling man because she felt so out of control?

God, she hoped not. But there was no time to mull over the past. She'd reached Drakon's side and felt another electric jolt as his gaze met hers and held. She couldn't look away from the warmth in his amber eyes. Part of him still burned and it made her want to burn with him. Madness, she told herself, don't go there, don't lose yourself, and yet the air hummed with heat and desire.

How could she not respond to him?

How could she not want to be close to him when he was so fiercely alive?

"It's going to be all right," he murmured, his deep voice pitched so low only she could hear.

Her lovely, lovely man that made her feel like the most beautiful woman in the entire world. Her lovely, lovely man that had pushed her to the brink, and beyond, and he still didn't know...still had no idea where she'd been that first year after leaving him, or what had happened to her trying to separate herself from him.

Part of her wanted to tell him, and yet another part didn't want to give him that knowledge, or power. Because he could break her. Absolutely destroy her. And she wasn't strong enough yet to rebuild herself again...not yet. Not on top of everything else that had happened to her father and her family with the Amery scandal.

"I promise you," he added.

She heard his fierce resolve and her heart turned over. This is how she'd fallen in love with him—his strength, his focus, his determination. That and the way he smiled at her... as if she were sunshine and oxygen all rolled into one. "Yes," she murmured, aware that once upon a time he'd been everything to her...her hope, her happiness, her future. She missed those days. Missed feeling as if she belonged somewhere with someone.

There was a flicker in his eyes, and then he made the introductions. "Morgan, this is Rowan Argyros, of Dunamas. Rowan, my wife, Morgan Copeland Xanthis."

Morgan forced her attention from Drakon to the stranger and her jaw nearly dropped. *This* was Rowan Argyros? *This* was one of the founders of Dunamas Maritime Intelligence?

Her brows tugged. She couldn't mask her surprise. Argyros wasn't at all what she'd expected.

She'd imagined Drakon's intelligence expert to look like one, and she'd pictured a man in his forties, maybe early fifties, who was stocky, balding, with a square jaw and pugilistic nose.

Instead Rowan Argyros looked like a model straight off some Parisian runway. He was gorgeous. Not her type at all, but her sister Logan would bed him in a heartbeat.

Tall and broad-shouldered, Argyros was muscular without any bulk. He was very tan, and his eyes were light, a pale gray or green, hard to know exactly in the diffused light of the ballroom. His dark brown hair was sun-streaked and he wore it straight and far too long for someone in his line of work. His jaw was strong, but not the thick bulldog jaw she'd come to associate with testosterone-driven males, but more angular...elegant, the kind of face that would photograph beautifully, although today that jaw was shadowed with a day-old beard.

"Mrs. Xanthis," Rowan said, extending a hand to her.

It bothered her that he hadn't even bothered to shave for their meeting, and she wondered how this could be the man who would free her father?

Rowan Argosy looked as if he'd spent his free time hanging out on obscenely big yachts off the coast of France, not planning daring, dangerous life-saving missions.

She shook his hand firmly and let it go quickly. "Mr. Argyros," she said crisply. "I would love to know what you know about my father. Drakon said you have information."

"I do," Rowan said, looking her straight in the eye, his voice hard, his expression as cool and unfriendly as hers.

Morgan's eyebrows lifted. Nice. She liked his frosty tone, and found his coldness and aloofness reassuring. She wouldn't have trusted him at all if he'd been warm and charming. Military types...intelligence types...they weren't the touchy-feely sort. "Is he alive?"

"He is. I have some film of him taken just this morning."

"How did you get it?"

"Does it matter?"

"No." And her legs felt like Jell-O and she took a step back, sitting down heavily in one of the chairs grouped behind them. Her heart was thudding so hard and fast she thought she might be sick and she drew great gulps of air, fighting waves of nausea and intense relief. Dad was alive. That was huge. "Thank God."

For a moment there was just silence as Morgan sat with the news, overwhelmed that her father was indeed alive. After a moment, when she could trust herself to speak, she looked up at Rowan. "And he's well? He's healthy?"

He hesitated. "We don't know that. We only have his location, and evidence that he is alive."

So Dad could be sick. He probably didn't have his heart medicine with him. It'd probably been left behind on his boat. "What happens now?" she asked.

"We get your father out, take him to wherever you want him to go."

"How does that happen, though?"

"We're going to have you call your contact, the one in Somalia you've been dealing with, and you're going to ask to speak to your father. You'll tell them you need proof that he's alive and well if they are to get the six million dollars."

"They won't let me speak to him. I tried that before."

"They will," Drakon interjected, arms folded across his chest, the shirt molded to his sculpted torso, "if they think you're ready to make a drop of six million."

She looked at him. "What if they call our bluff? Wouldn't we have to be prepared to make the drop?"

"Yes. And we will. We'll give them a date, a time, co-ordinates for the drop. We'll tell them who is making the drop, too."

"But we're not dropping any money, are we?" she asked, glancing from him to Rowan and back again.

"No," said Rowan. "We're preparing a team right now to move in and rescue your father. But speaking to your father gives us important information, as well as buys us a little more time to put our plan in place."

She nodded, processing this. "How long until you rescue him?"

"Soon. Seventy-two hours, or less."

She looked at Rowan, startled. "That is soon."

"Once we have our plan in place, it's better to strike fast." Rowan's phone made a low vibrating noise and he reached into his pocket and checked the number. "I need to take this call," he said, walking away.

Morgan exhaled as Rowan exited through the sunroom, into the stairwell that would take him back up to the main level of the villa.

"You okay?" Drakon asked, looking down on her, after Rowan disappeared.

"Things can go wrong," she said.

"Yes. And sometimes they do. But Dunamas has an impressive track record. Far more successes than failures. I wouldn't have enlisted their help if I didn't think they'd succeed."

She hesitated. "If Rowan's team didn't succeed...people could die."

"People *will* die even if they do succeed. They're planning a raid. The pirates are heavily armed. Dunamas's team will be heavily armed. It's not going to be a peaceful handover. It'll be explosive and violent, and yet the team they're sending are professionals. They're prepared to do whatever they have to do to get him out alive."

So some of them—or all of them—could end up dying for her father?

Nauseated all over again, Morgan moved from her chair, not wanting to think of the brave, battle-tested men, men the world viewed as heroic, risking their lives for her father, who wasn't a hero.

Stomach churning, she pushed open one of the sunroom's tall arched glass doors and stepped onto the terrace, into the sunshine. She drank in a breath of fresh air, and then another. Was she being selfish, trying to save her father? Should she not do this?

Panic and guilt buffeted her as she leaned against the terrace's creamy marble balustrade and squeezed her eyes closed.

Drakon had followed her outside. "What's wrong?"

She didn't answer immediately, trying to find the right words, but what were those words? How did one make a decision like this? "Am I doing the wrong thing?" she asked. "Am I wrong, trying to save him?"

"I can't answer that for you. He's your father. Your family."

"You know I tried everything before I came to you. I asked everyone for help. No one would help me."

"Who did you approach?"

"Who didn't I?" She laughed grimly and glanced out across the terraced gardens with the roses and hedges and the pool and the view of the sea beyond. "I went to London to see Branson, and then to Los Angeles to see Logan, and then to Tori in New York, and back to London, but none of them would contribute money toward Dad's ransom. They're all in tight financial straits, and they all have reasons they couldn't give, but I think they wouldn't contribute to the ransom because they're ashamed of Dad. I think they believe I'm wasting money trying to rescue him. Mom even said he's better off where he is…that people will find it easier to forgive us—his kids—if Dad doesn't come back."

"You mean, if the pirates kill him?" Drakon asked.

She nodded.

"Your mother is probably right," he said.

She shot him a swift glance before pushing away from the railing to pace the length of the terrace. For a long minute she just walked, trying to master her emotions. "Maybe," she said, "maybe Mom is right, but I don't care. I don't care what people think of me. I don't care if they like me. I care about what's right. And while what Dad did, just blindly giving Michael the money, wasn't right, it's also not right to leave him in Somalia. And maybe the others can write him off, but I can't."

She shivered, chilled, even though the sun was shining warmly overhead. "I can't forget how he taught me to swim and ride a bike and he went to every one of my volleyball games in high school. Dad was there for everything, big and small, and maybe he was a terrible investment advisor, but he was a wonderful father. I couldn't have asked for better—" Morgan broke off, covering her mouth to stifle a sob. She couldn't help it, but she missed him, and worried about him, and there was just no way she could turn her back on him now. No way at all.

"I think you have your answer," Drakon said quietly. "You have to do this. Have to help him. Right or wrong."

They both turned at the sound of a squeaky gate. Rowan was heading up toward them from the lower garden.

"And if anybody can get your father home, it's Argyros," Drakon said.

Morgan wrinkled her nose. "He looks like a drug smuggler."

The corner of Drakon's mouth lifted. "He isn't what one expects. That's what makes him so successful."

"As long as you trust him."

"I do."

On reaching their side, Rowan announced that his office was now ready for Morgan to try to phone her pirate contact in Somalia. "We have a special line set up that will allow us to record the conversation," he said. "And my team is standing by now, to listen in on the call."

"But I can only use my phone," she answered. "And my number. They know my number—"

"We know. And we can make it appear to look like your number. Today's technology lets us do just about anything."

In the villa's dark-paneled library they attempted the call but no one answered on the other end. Morgan left a message, letting her contact know that she had six million in cash, in used bills, and was ready to make the drop but she wanted to speak to her father first. "I need to know he's alive," she said, "and then you'll have the money."

She hung up, glanced at Rowan and Drakon. "And now what?"

"We wait for a call back," Rowan said.

They had a light lunch in the library while waiting, but there was no return call. Morgan wanted to phone again but Rowan said it wasn't a good idea. "We're playing a game," he explained. "It's their game, but we're going to outplay them. They just don't know it yet."

The afternoon dragged. Morgan hated waiting as it made her restless and anxious. She wanted to hear her father's voice, and she wanted to hear it sooner than later. After a couple hours, she couldn't sit still any longer and began to walk in circles. She saw Morgan and Drakon exchange glances.

"What?" she demanded. "Am I not allowed to move out of my chair?"

Drakon smiled faintly. "Come, let's go get some exercise and fresh air."

Stretching her legs did sound nice, but Morgan didn't want to miss the call. "What if the pirate calls back and I'm not here?"

"He'll leave a message," Drakon said.

"Won't he be angry?" she asked.

Rowan shrugged. "They want your money. They'll call back."

It was close to four when Morgan and Drakon left the house to walk down to the water, and the afternoon was still bright, and warm, but already the sun was sitting lower in the sky. Morgan took a deep breath, glad to have escaped the dark cool library and be back outside.

"Thank you for getting me out of there," she said to Drakon as they crossed the lawn, heading for the stone and cement staircase that hugged the cliff and took them down to the little dock, where they used to anchor the speedboat they used to explore the coast.

"You were looking a little pale in there," Drakon said, walking next to her. "But your father's going to be all right."

"If I was pale, it's because I was thinking about what we did earlier." Her fingers knotted into fists. "Or what we shouldn't have done." She glanced up at him as he opened the second wrought-iron gate, this one at the top of the stairs.

"Which was?" he asked innocently.

She shot him a disbelieving look and his golden brown eyes sparked, the corner of his sexy mouth tugging in a slow, wicked smile and just like that the air was suddenly charged, and Morgan shivered at the sudden snap and crackle of tension and the spike of awareness. God, it was electric between them. And dangerous.

"It can't happen again," she whispered, her gaze meeting his.

"No?" he murmured, reaching out to lift a soft tendril of hair back from her cheek, but then he couldn't let it go and he let the strand slide between his fingers, before curling it loosely around his finger and thumb.

Her breath caught in her throat and she stared up at him, heart pounding, mouth drying. She loved the way he touched her and he was making her weak in the knees now. "It confuses me."

"Confuses you, how?"

The heat between them was intense. Dizzying. So much awareness, so much desire, so impossible to satisfy. She swayed on her feet and he immediately stepped between her and the edge of the stairs, pressing her up against the wall. "I can't think around you," she whispered, feeling his dazzling energy before her, and the sun warmed rock at her back.

"Thinking is overrated," he murmured, moving in closer to her, brushing his lips across her forehead.

She closed her eyes, breathing in his light clean fragrance and savoring the teasing caress. "Is it?"

"Mmm-hmm."

"Does that mean you're not going to think, either?"

She felt the corners of his mouth curve against her brow. He was smiling. And God, didn't that turn her on?

She locked her knees, her inner thighs clenching, wanting him, needing. Damn him.

"One of us should probably keep our heads," he answered, his hands cupping her face, thumbs stroking her cheekbones. "Less frantic that way."

"And I suppose you think that should be you?" she breathed, trying to resist the pleasure of his hands pushing deep into her hair, his fingers wrapping around the strands, his knuckles grazing her scalp. He was so good at turning her on, making her feel, and he was making her feel now with a little tug, a touch, and just like that, desire rushed through her...hot, consuming, intense.

"Of course," he said, leaning in to her, his mouth lightly kissing down from her brow, over her cheekbone, to the soft swell of her lips.

"Why?"

"Because no one has ever loved you the way I loved you."

Her eyes flew open and she stared into his eyes. "Don't say that."

"It's true. You know how I feel about you. You know I cannot refuse you anything."

"Not true. For five years you refused to grant me the divorce."

"Because I didn't want to lose you."

"Five years is a long time to wait for someone."

"I would have waited forever for you, Morgan."

Her heart was pounding again, even harder. "That doesn't make sense, Drakon. Nothing about this...us...makes sense."

"Who said love was supposed to make sense?"

She exhaled hard, in a quick, desperate rush, and she had to blink hard to clear her vision. "Did you *really* love me?"

"How can you doubt it?"

She frowned, thinking, trying to remember. Why had she doubted it? Why had she not felt loved? How did she get from besotted bride to runaway wife?

He reached out, tipped her chin up, so he could look deeper into her eyes. "Morgan, tell me. How could you doubt me?"

"Because after our honeymoon...after we left here...I didn't feel loved...." Her voice drifted off as she struggled to piece it together. How lost she'd felt in Athens, how confused waiting for him all day, needing him so much that when he walked through the door, she didn't know if she should run to him, or hide, ashamed for feeling so empty. "But then, after a while, I didn't feel anything anymore—" She broke off, bit down into her lip, piercing the skin. "No, that's not true. I did feel something. I felt crazy, Drakon. I felt crazy living with you."

"Don't say that."

"It's true."

He stepped away from her, turned and faced the sea, then rubbed his palm across the bristles on his jaw.

Morgan watched him just long enough to see the pain in his eyes. She'd hurt him. Again.

Hating herself, hating what they did to each other, she slipped past him and continued down the stairs to the water's edge.

She had to get out of here. And she had to get out of here soon.

CHAPTER EIGHT

HE SWORE SOFTLY, and shook his head.

God, that woman was frustrating. And to think he hadn't just fallen in love with her, but he'd married her.

Married her.

Long before his wedding day, Drakon had been warned by other men that getting married changed things. He'd been warned that wives—and marriage—were a lot of work. But Drakon hadn't been daunted. He didn't mind work. He'd succeeded because he'd always worked hard, put in long hours, never expecting life to be easy.

But marriage to Morgan hadn't started out difficult. It'd been amazing initially. She'd been amazing, and everything had been easy, since Morgan had been easiness herself...joyful, uncomplicated, undemanding. And then they moved into the new villa in Ekali, the affluent Athens neighborhood, and she'd changed...expressing worries, and then doubts, and then needs which came to sound like demands.

Be home from work early.

Don't work too late.

Why aren't you ever here?

And if he were honest, he had worked long hours, really long hours, and the more Morgan pressured him to come home, the more he wanted to be at the office, and he'd told himself he was working late to provide for her, working late to ensure she had everything she needed, when deep inside he knew he was just avoiding going home to her. It wasn't that he didn't love her...but he was suddenly so aware of how she now depended on him for everything. It overwhelmed him. How could he meet all those needs? How could he manage her, and his work, and his responsibilities?

While he grew more distant, she grew more emotional, her sunny smiles fading until they were gone, replaced by a woman who looked fragile and haunted, her eyes sad, her lovely face taut, her expression stricken.

It made him angry, this change in her. Made him angry that she couldn't be like his other women...happy to shop and visit salons and spas and just enjoy being spoiled, enjoy the prestige of being Drakon Xanthis's pampered wife. It was good enough for his other women. Why not for her?

Why did Morgan want more? More to the point, what did she want from *him?*

He'd never told her—or anyone—but in his mind, she'd become like his mother. Drakon loved his mother, he was a dutiful son, but he didn't want to be around her, and that's what happened with Morgan. Morgan made him feel inadequate and he dealt with it by avoiding her.

And then one day Morgan disappeared, abruptly returning to America, and he had exploded.

How could she have just walk away from him like that? How could she give up? How *dare* she give up? He hadn't been happy all those years ago, but he hadn't walked away from her. He hadn't felt the magic, either, but he wasn't a quitter—

And then it struck him. He had quit on her. Maybe he hadn't physically left, but he'd checked out emotionally.

And only now he could see that her needs hadn't been so overwhelming. She hadn't asked for that much. But the fact that she'd asked for anything—time, tenderness, reassurance—had triggered the worst in him, and he'd reacted like the boy he'd once been, retreating, hiding, rejecting.

He'd given her money but not affection.

He'd given her toys but not his heart.

He'd given her stuff...as long as she didn't engage him, want him, need him. Don't bother him because he couldn't, wouldn't, deal with anyone else's problems—he had plenty of his own.

Ah.

And there it was. The ugly, ugly truth.

Drakon Xanthis was a selfish, shallow, stunted man. A man that looked strong on the outside but was just an angry child on the inside. And that's when he knew, that he'd wronged Morgan...badly. Cruelly. He'd taken a twenty-two-year-old woman from her home and her country and dropped her into his white marble house and told her to be silent and to not feel and to not need. To not express emotion, to not reach out, to not cry, to not talk, to not be human.

My God.

He'd done to her what his mother had done to him. Be there, Drakon, but do not need. Be present, Drakon, but do not feel....

Five years ago Drakon went in search of Morgan, seeking to right the wrongs, but she was gone. She'd vanished...completely disappeared...and his anger with himself grew. He'd loved Morgan and he'd treated her so badly. He'd taken the person who loved him, wanted him, the real him—the man, not the name, the bank account, the status—and crushed her.

He'd broken her.

He knew it. And all he'd wanted was to find her, apologize, fix everything. And he couldn't. Morgan was gone again. And Drakon was shattered. Until she came back, until he could make things right, he was a man in hell.

Now, from the top of the stairs, he watched Morgan step onto the platform down below, her brown hair gleaming in the sunlight, spilling down her back. His chest hurt, heavy and aching with suppressed emotion.

Morgan. His woman. His.

She stood on the platform, a hand shadowing her eyes as she looked out across the water. A wooden rowboat, the color of a robin's egg, was tethered to the platform and bobbed next to her. The blue rowboat, and dark sapphire sea, perfectly framed Morgan in her fitted white dress, which accented her slim curves.

She looked fresh and young standing on the platform, and when she slipped off her shoes and sat down on the pier's edge, pulling her crisp skirts high on her thigh so that she could put her bare feet in the water, he felt a fierce surge of emotion.

It had been his job to love her, cherish her and protect her. And he'd failed in all three counts.

Watching her, Drakon's chest grew tight. He'd vowed five years ago to make things right, and he hadn't made them right yet. Giving her a check and a divorce wasn't right. It was easy. Easier to let her go than to change, or struggle to save them. But he didn't want easy. He wanted Morgan. And she was worth fighting for, and she was worth changing for, and she was worth everything to him.

She was everything to him.

He'd known it the moment he'd lost her.

And now that she was here, he realized that he could not give up on her. Could not give up on them. Not because he needed to win her back, not because he needed to prove anything—for God's sake, he was Drakon Xanthis, and the world was his oyster—but because he loved *her,* Morgan Copeland.

And for the past five years, Morgan Copeland had tied him up in knots. But he was a smart man. He could figure out how to untie the knots. He could figure out how to reach her, how to make this—them—work.

It was a challenge, but he liked challenges. He'd never been afraid of tackling difficult situations. What was it that his father used to say? Problems were just opportunities in disguise?

Morgan being here was an opportunity. And Drakon would make the most of the opportunity.

"It was a mistake making love without protection," Drakon said quietly. "And I accept full responsibility should you get pregnant."

Morgan stiffened. She hadn't heard Drakon approach, but now she felt him there behind her, and her nape prickled, the hair on her arms lifted, and a shiver raced through her as she remembered how it felt being with him in her room, his skin on her skin, his mouth taking hers, his body giving her so much pleasure.

It had been so good. So intense and physical that she lost perspective. Forgot what was important. But then, hadn't that always been his effect on her?

"What does that mean?" she asked quietly, reaching up to pluck a fine strand of hair away from her eyelashes as she kept her gaze fixed on the watery horizon, where the sunlight shimmered in every direction. "That you will accept full responsibility if I get pregnant?"

"I'll assume full financial responsibility, for you and the child, and once the baby is born, I will assume full physical custody of the child—"

"What?" she choked, cutting him short as she turned to look at him where he was standing on the narrow stair landing behind her, leaning against the rock wall. "You'll take my baby?"

"Our baby," he calmly corrected, broad shoulders shifting, "and I am quite able to raise a child on my own, Morgan. I will get help, of course, but I'll be a good father—"

"You'd take the baby away from me?"

"If that would make you feel better—"

"It wouldn't."

"You said earlier that you didn't want to be a single mother."

"I don't. It wouldn't be right for the baby. But that doesn't mean you can have him or her."

He walked toward her. "But I'm ready to be a father, and you're not wanting to be a mother right now—"

"You can't say that. You don't know that. My God, Drakon! Where are you getting this from?"

"First of all, right now, as far as we know, there's no baby. And secondly, *should* you conceive, then of course I'd want to support my child—financially, emotionally, physically. I won't be an absentee father."

Her skin prickled as he stood above her. The man was pure electricity. The air practically pulsed with energy. "No, I don't want to be pregnant right now, it's not high on my to-do list at the moment, with my father being held hostage and my family in chaos, but if I was pregnant, I'd manage."

"That's not good enough. My child deserves better than that. If you are pregnant, we'll have to do the right thing for our child, which means raising him or her in a calm, stable home, without chaos."

"Then you'd be stuck with me, Drakon, because I'm not handing over my child."

"Our child."

"Which might not even exist."

"Which probably doesn't exist, because when we were newlyweds and having unprotected sex every day, twice a day, for months, you didn't get pregnant."

She bit into her lip, hating the panic rushing through here. This was just a conversation of hypotheticals. "Does that mean if I do conceive, you'd want the baby and me to live with you?"

"Yes."

It's not real, she reminded herself, don't freak out. "And we'd be divorced?"

"No."

"No?"

He shook his head. "Absolutely not. If you're pregnant, we'll stay together. If you're not, I'll have my attorney file the divorce papers. But as we won't know that for a couple more weeks, I won't have my attorney file until we know for certain."

"Awfully convenient," she muttered under her breath.

"Happily so," he answered, not rising to the bait. "This way there would be no stigma attached to the child. We're still legally married. The baby would be a result of our reconciliation."

"And if I'm not pregnant?"

"You'll be free—single—within a couple months."

Morgan didn't immediately speak. Instead she looked out across the water and listened to the waves break and felt the breeze catch and lift her hair. She might appear calm, but her thoughts were tangled and her emotions intense. "And should the unthinkable happen, should I conceive...we would all live together, as a family?"

"Yes."

She turned to look at him. "Where would we raise the baby?"

"Greece," he said firmly.

She made a rough sound, tucking a strand of hair behind her ear. "I'd prefer not to raise a child in Greece."

"Why not?"

"I don't like Greece."

"How can you not like Greece? It's beautiful and warm and so full of life."

"I found it excruciatingly isolating, and horribly boring—"

"There was no reason for you to be bored. You had money, a driver, you could have gone shopping. The salesclerks would have loved you. They would have waited on you hand and foot."

Battling her temper, Morgan drew her feet out of the water,

wrapped her arms around bent knees. "Not all women live to shop."

"Most women do."

"You can't generalize like that. It's not true." He started to protest and she overrode him. "Obviously one or more of your past girlfriends managed to convince you that retail therapy was the answer for everything, but I'm not one of them." She rose to her feet. "Shopping when I'm lonely just makes me feel worse...wandering alone from store to store looking for something to buy...how pathetic is that?"

"It would have been better than you sitting sulking at home."

Heat rushed through her, and her cheeks suddenly burned. "Sulking? Shopping? Why in God's name did you even marry shallow, materialistic me?"

"You were young. I thought you'd change."

"I can't believe you just said that! I can't believe you think you're so perfect...that you had no blame in our failed marriage."

"So what did I do wrong?" he asked.

"You didn't talk to me."

He laughed. "*That's* my mistake?"

Her eyes blazed. "Fine, laugh, but it's true. Our marriage ended because we didn't talk to each other. It ended because we both kept everything bottled inside and I think it's time we started talking, and saying those things that aren't comfortable, but true—"

"It's not going to change anything."

"No, but at least it'll clear the air. Perhaps give us better understanding of what happened...maybe help me understand you."

"Me?" he said incredulously. "What is there to understand about me?"

"Everything! I married one person and yet I ended up with another."

He drew back, shocked. "I didn't change. Morgan, it was you. When we married, you were strong and confident, and then before I knew what happened, you turned into an angry, silent woman who only responded when I touched her. So I touched you, as often as I could, as much as I could, trying to get you back."

"Words would have worked. Words and conversation."

"I don't trust words. Don't put much stock in conversation."

"Obviously, but would it have killed you to ask me about my day, or tell me about your day—" She broke off, averting her head, unable to look at him when her heart felt so bruised and tender. What a mistake it had been…falling in love… thinking it would work. "Let's just hope I'm not pregnant," she added hoarsely. "Because I don't want to go through life like this, trying to explain myself, trying to be accepted, only to be mocked by you."

Drakon shook his head, muttering something under his breath, something with quite a few syllables and from his inflection, sounded far from flattering.

"What did you just say?" she demanded.

"Doesn't matter."

"No, it does. I want to hear this. I want to hear everything you wouldn't tell me before."

"You gave up on us so quickly, Morgan. You didn't give yourself time to adjust to married life, nor did you try to make friends."

"Maybe I did give up too soon, but you could have tried to help me adjust to Athens. Instead you dropped me off at the house and expected me to keep myself busy until you returned every night."

"I had a job to do."

"You could have made more of an effort to help me adjust. You could have taken the time to show me around, or cut your day short now and then so we could take a walk, or visit a nearby beach, or even have people over."

Drakon looked bewildered. "Have people over? For what?"

"Have dinner, visit, socialize." She could see by his expression that he still didn't get it. "Surely, you're used to entertaining...having some friends over for a barbecue or a party."

"To my house?"

"Yes."

"Never have."

"Why not?"

"My family didn't. I never did. I don't have time, nor is it something I'd want to do. I work long days, and when I go home, I want to relax, rest, focus on what I need to do the next day."

"But while you were working twelve- and fourteen-hour days, Drakon, what was I supposed to do?"

"Read a book...take language courses...learn to cook?" He shrugged, sighed, running a hand through his cropped dark hair. "Eventually we would have had children. And then, of course, you had the house."

"The *house?*" Morgan suppressed a sudden urge to throw rocks at his head. "Did you actually just say I had the *house?*"

"Yes, the house. The one I had built for you."

"You did not build that marble mausoleum for me. You bought it for me—"

"No, I bought the lot, scrapped the old house that was there and built our home for you."

"I *hated* the villa."

"What?"

Her eyebrows lifted, her lips twisting. "Yes. I hated it. It's awful. It was too white and sterile, never mind cold, modern and boxy—"

"It's a ten-million-dollar architectural masterpiece, Morgan."

"Or merely an outrageously expensive ice cube tray!"

His eyes sparked. "You disappoint me."

"Yes, so I've gathered. You work twelve-hour days while I'm home learning Greek, and how to cook, and hopefully getting pregnant." She shuddered. "What a horrendous life that would have been. Thank God I escaped when I did!"

He reached out, his fingers wrapping around her bicep to haul her against him. "Do you know how many women would be thrilled to live in that house?"

"I have no idea, although I'm sure Bronwyn would love to be one." She flung her head back to look him in the eye. "How is she, by the way? Doing well?"

"She's fine."

"I bet she is."

"What does that mean?"

"What do you think it means, Drakon?"

"I think it means you're petty and irrational when it comes to Bron. She's never been anything but polite to you—"

"Give me a break!"

"—ordering you flowers, arranging for your birthday cake," he continued, as if she'd never interrupted.

Morgan shook his hand off her arm. "How nice of her to get me flowers from you and order birthday cake for me. It makes me feel so good to know that your vice president of Southeast Asia was able to do those little things to make my birthday special since you were too busy to do it yourself."

He tensed and his jaw popped. "That's not why I didn't do it."

"No? Then why didn't you do it?" She dragged in a breath of air, holding it a moment, fighting for control, not wanting to cry now. She would not cry while discussing Bronwyn. Would not lose it now when she needed to be strong. "Because I didn't want flowers picked out by the woman who is spending all day at the office with you. I didn't want a cake ordered by her, either. She's not my friend. She's not my family. She doesn't like me and is only trying to get closer to you."

"She was doing me a favor."

"Ah. I knew it. It was about you."

"What does that mean?"

"It means, that her favor to you, was not just unnecessary, but it actually hurt me."

"That's ridiculous."

And this was why she and Drakon weren't together. This was why she'd left him, and this was why they'd never be together.

Even though part of her would always love him, they couldn't be together, because outside the bedroom, they simply didn't work. There was no real understanding, no meeting of the minds. The only time they connected, the only time they made sense, was when they were having sex. But sex was just a part of a relationship, it couldn't be the relationship.

She looked up at him, her expression fierce. "Perhaps you will permit me to give you a little advice. Maybe I can do something for the future Mrs. Xanthis. Don't let Bronwyn, or any other woman, intrude so much in your personal life. The women you work with shouldn't be allowed to overshadow the woman you live with. And should you want to send your wife flowers, or a gift, do it yourself or don't do it at all."

His eyes glittered and he looked almost pale beneath his tan. "Anything else, Morgan?"

"Yes, actually. Next time you marry, ask your bride what kind of home she wants to live in. Or better yet, include her on the design process, or take her with you when you go house hunting. That way your poor wife might actually like her cage."

"Cage?" he choked out, expression furious.

She shrugged, shoulders twisting. "It's what it felt like," she said, slipping past him to climb the stone and cement stairs that led back up to the house. And then halfway up the staircase, she paused. "But I'm not your pet, Drakon, and I won't be kept!"

And then with her skirts in her hands, she raced on up, half hoping he'd follow and end this terrible fight the only way they knew how to end things—through sex.

Because right now she wanted him and needed him, not to make her come, but to make her feel safe. Sane. Only she didn't know how to ask him for comfort, and he didn't know how to give comfort. Just raw, carnal pleasure.

But even raw, carnal pleasure would be better than nothing right now, and as she continued up toward the house, she tried not to think how good it'd feel to have him push her back against the rock wall and capture her hands in his and hold her immobile all the while kissing her senseless, kissing her until she was wet and ready for him and he could take her here, in the sun, near the sea, with the tang of salt in her nose and the sweet heady fragrance of jasmine perfuming the air, and the taste of Drakon—her husband, and her heart—on her tongue.

CHAPTER NINE

THERE WAS NO call back from the pirates and Morgan spent the rest of the afternoon in her bedroom. She didn't have to stay in her room, but she thought it safer than wandering around the villa or the extensive grounds, where she might bump into Drakon.

In her room, Morgan tried napping and she actually fell asleep, but didn't sleep long, as her mother called, waking her. It was a brief, meaningless conversation about social events and it infuriated Morgan that her mother would even ask, much less expect, Morgan to drop everything to attend a charity fund-raiser with her.

"I'm in Italy working to bring Dad home," Morgan told her mother.

"No one is going to give you the money, Morgan." Her mother paused. "And if they do, they are fools."

After hanging up, Morgan tried to fall back asleep, but she couldn't, too unsettled from the call. So she took a long bath, trying to forget the things her mother said, remaining in the tub until the water turned cold and the skin on her fingers shriveled up.

Morgan was chilled by the time she got out of the bath, and she blew her hair dry and dressed carefully for dinner, trying to fill her time, trying to stay busy so she wouldn't go find Drakon.

She wanted Drakon. She missed him. Didn't want to be

at the villa with him and yet not with him. The last time she was here, on that delicious, luxurious honeymoon, they spent almost every moment together and it didn't seem right being at the villa and not seeing him.

But then, life didn't seem right without him in it.

But finally, thankfully, she'd managed to get through the afternoon and now it was almost dinner, and time for the nightly *aperitivo.*

Morgan was the first to the living room for the Italian *aperitivo.* The pre-dinner drink was a tradition at Villa An-gelica, one she and Drakon had come to enjoy during their honeymoon.

In the living room, Morgan went to the antique table that had been set up as the bar with a selection of alcohol and juices, sodas, sparkling water and tonic water and other cock-tail mixes. Morgan bypassed the mixes for the pitcher of Campari. Tonight it was Campari with pomegranate. Tomor-row night it might be Campari orange. The cocktail changed every night and Morgan enjoyed sampling the different vari-ations.

She wandered now with her cocktail to the window to watch the sunset. It would be another stunning sunset and the sky was a fiery red orange at the moment and she sipped the cocktail, basking in the warm rays of the sun reaching through the glass.

This was like a dream, she thought, one of those dreams she had when she was at McLean Hospital, when she'd dream of Drakon every night, and in her dreams they were together still, and happy...so very, very happy....

Suddenly footsteps sounded in the stairwell and Morgan turned to watch Drakon descend the final flight of stairs and step into the grand entry. Her heart turned over in her chest as she watched him. He moved with such ease, and so much grace, that he made other men look clumsy. But then, he'd al-ways had confidence, and a physicality that other men didn't have. She'd wondered if growing up on boats, working on cargo ships as if he were a deckhand instead of the owner's son, had given him that awareness and balance.

As he crossed the hall and joined her in the living room, the enormous Venetian chandelier bathed him in light and she sucked in a breath, struck all over again by his intensity and that strong, hard face with those intensely observant eyes.

He was looking at her now. She grew warm under his inspection, remembering how much she'd wanted to go to him earlier, how much she'd craved him all afternoon.

"Hello," she said, hoping he couldn't see her blush.

"Hello," he answered, the corner of his mouth quirking as if amused.

His smile did something to her and she felt a frisson of pleasure race through her. Flustered, Morgan lifted her drink to her lips, sipped her cocktail and studied Drakon covertly over the rim of her glass. He was wearing a crisp white dress shirt open at the collar and fine trousers and he looked like the Drakon she'd married—polished, elegant, handsome— but she'd learned something new about him during the last twenty-four hours. He wasn't as controlled as she'd imagined. If anything he was a man of passion.

And that was both good and bad. Good, because he met her intensity and answered her fierce need for touch and sensation. Bad, because soon he'd be out of her life again and she couldn't imagine ever feeling this way about any other man. Couldn't imagine ever wanting any other man.

"Were you able to get a nap?" he asked, turning away to pour himself a drink.

He, too, chose the Campari cocktail and for some reason that made her happy. "I did lie down," Morgan answered, her back now to the window so she could face Drakon, "but the moment I finally fell asleep, my phone rang. It was my mother."

"Calling to get news about your father?"

"No. She just wanted to know if I'd be home to attend a fund-raiser in Greenwich with her this weekend." Morgan shook her head incredulously. "A black-tie fund-raiser! Can you imagine?"

"You used to attend events like that all the time."

"Yes, when we were socially desirable, but we're not anymore. We're hated, loathed, but Mom doesn't get it. She's trying to carry on as if everything is the same, but nothing's the same. Only Mom refuses to face facts, refuses to accept that no one wants us at their balls or parties or fund-raisers anymore." Morgan tried to laugh but couldn't quite pull it off. "Dad's being held hostage in Somalia and Mom's trying to find a date for this Saturday's symphony gala. What a horrible family you married into, Drakon!"

His amber gaze suddenly locked with hers. "I didn't marry them. I married you."

"And I'm the craziest of them all!"

He said nothing for a long moment and then he smiled, a slow, wicked smile that put an equally wicked gleam in his eye. "Is that why sex was always so much fun?"

She blushed but was saved from answering by the sudden appearance of Rowan. "Your contact from Somalia just phoned," he said, entering the living room. "He left a message. They're not going to let you speak with your father. But since you have the money ready, they want to arrange the drop, and give you instructions on where you'll find your hostage."

Morgan's smile died on her lips and she glanced at Drakon, and then back at Rowan. "Did they really say it like that?"

Rowan nodded and Morgan paled and swallowed hard. "They make my father sound like a carcass," she whispered, sickened.

"We're not dealing with sensitive people," Rowan answered.

"But don't panic," Drakon added. "I'm sure he's still alive."

She drew a quick breath and lifted her chin. "I want him out of there."

"He will be," Drakon said.

Rowan nodded. "Soon.

It took them a while to move from the living room to the dining room for dinner, but once they got there, the dining room glowed with candlelight. The dining room's antique chandelier was filled with tapers, and the iron and glass sconces on the white walls reflected onto the ceiling making every surface gleam and dance with light. But the meal was definitely subdued. Morgan was both angry and heartsick and felt impossibly distracted. Rowan barely spoke and Drakon didn't say much more than Rowan. But every now and then Morgan looked up to find Drakon watching her, his expression shuttered and impossible to read.

Perhaps if she and Drakon had been alone, she would have asked him what he was thinking, but with Rowan present, Morgan left Drakon to his own thoughts, and she tried not to dwell on her father, or his conditions in Somalia.

As Drakon said, her father would be home soon. Rowan had agreed with him.

She had to focus on that, cling to that, not allow herself to slide into panic or doubt.

Finally the dinner dishes were being cleared away and coffee was served. But sitting in silence with coffee proved even more uncomfortable than eating in silence.

"I hate them," she choked out, unable to remain silent another moment. "I hate how they've taken him and are treating him like he's nothing...nobody...just an object to be bartered."

"It is horrendous," Drakon agreed quietly.

"But it's on the rise, isn't it?" She looked up at him as she added another half teaspoon of sugar to her coffee and gave it a brisk stir. "From what I read, attacks have doubled in the last few years."

Drakon's dark head inclined. "Last year there were more hostages taken than ever before."

"Nearly twelve hundred," Morgan murmured, having done a fair amount of research on her own, trying to understand what had happened to her father. "With many being held for nine months or more. Unthinkable. But it's real. It's happening."

"At least your father will be freed," Rowan said brusquely. "There are hundreds of hostages who haven't been ransomed...that will never be ransomed."

Morgan's insides twisted. She couldn't imagine being one of the unfortunate crew who were never freed. How terrible to sit day after day, week after week, month after month waiting for a ransom that might never come. "Because someone isn't willing to pay the ransom?" she asked.

"Or able to pay it. Not all shipping companies have insurance that will pay it, and most ordinary people can't come up with millions of dollars, not even to save a loved one," Drakon answered.

Morgan put her spoon down, her eyes burning, guilt eating at her because she was able to help her father. She was able to do something and yet she felt for those who couldn't. "Fortunately, I understand the counter-piracy measures put in place this past year seem to be helping. From what I read, piracy was down during the first quarter of the year—not enough of course to give cause for celebration, but enough to know that the experts might be on to something."

"That's true," Drakon agreed. "Right now there's a concerted international effort to check piracy, and it's helping, but it certainly hasn't stopped the pirates. It's just slowed them a little."

"How do you stop them?"

"Put a stable, strong, and effective government in place.

Change their economic structure. Take out the group who is arming the pirates, and profiting from the hostage ransoms." Rowan's lips curved, his expression hard. "But if that were easy, it would have been done already. And so we do the next best thing—increase maritime intelligence and continue international cooperation on monitoring the water off the Horn of Africa."

"Until I began researching piracy I didn't realize that until recently, few countries worked together...that for the most part, most countries just focused on their own pirated vessels," Morgan answered.

Rowan shrugged. "Typical nationalistic reaction."

"How so?"

"Every country has its own navy, military intelligence and sources, so it's not easy getting everyone on the same page. Governments are protective of their military and don't want to share resources," he answered her.

Morgan frowned. "But you're military?"

"Former, yes. Just as most of us in maritime intelligence have served in one arm of the navy or another."

"Were you in the Royal Navy?" she asked.

"I've actually served in both the U.S. Navy and the Royal Navy, but at different times and in different capacities."

Morgan glanced to Drakon and then back to Rowan. "How is that possible?"

"I have dual nationalities...I was born in Northern Ireland to an Irish mother, and an American Greek father, giving me both American and British citizenship."

"Irish, too," Drakon said.

"They let you have all those passports?" Morgan asked, rather amazed.

Rowan shrugged. "If you're good at what you do."

"And you are good, I take it?"

His lips curved but the smile didn't reach his eyes. "Have

to be. There's a lot at stake—" He broke off as the sound of high heels clicking briskly on hard tiles echoed in the hallway.

They were all listening to the footsteps and Morgan stiffened, her shoulders drawing back as unease rolled through her in a huge dark wave.

Bronwyn.

Morgan went hot and then cold. But no, it couldn't be. What would Bronwyn be doing here?

And yet no one else walked that way. No one else sounded so fiercely confident in high stiletto heels.

Then there she was, appearing in the dining room doorway as if she owned Villa Angelica, as tall and blonde and statuesque as ever, dressed tonight in a formfitting red jersey knit that clung to her curves, making the most of her voluptuous body. Bronwyn, a stunning blonde with brilliant blue eyes and a dark golden tan, knew how to make an entrance.

"Hope I haven't kept you waiting," she said, smiling, as her gaze swept the dining room, before lingering on Drakon.

Morgan's stomach hurt as she saw the way Bronwyn looked at Drakon. Drakon had always said that Bronwyn was just part of his management team, a valuable employee and nothing more, but from the possessive expression on Bronwyn's face, Morgan knew that Bronwyn was fiercely attached to Drakon.

"You haven't kept us waiting," Drakon answered, rising and gesturing to a chair at the table. "Join us. Have you eaten? Would you like coffee? Something sweet?"

Bronwyn flashed Drakon a grateful smile as she moved around the dining room table to take an empty chair. "A glass of wine would be perfect. You know what I like."

Morgan ground her teeth together as she glanced from Bronwyn to Drakon and then back to Bronwyn again. How could he have invited her here, now, when they were in the middle of a crisis? How could he possibly think it was appropriate?

Bronwyn sat down and crossed one leg over the other, then gave her head a small toss, sending her long, artfully layered blond hair spilling over her shoulders down to the tops of her high full breasts. "Drakon, next time, send the helicopter for me, not a driver. I was nauseous from Sorrento on. Such a grueling drive. So many hairpin curves."

Drakon didn't respond; too busy speaking to one of the kitchen staff, requesting Bronwyn's wine.

Bronwyn turned to Rowan. "Haven't seen you in a while. How are you?"

"Busy," he answered flatly, expression hard.

"But it must be nice to be in a business that is booming," she retorted.

"Not if there are people's lives at stake," Morgan said, unable to remain silent.

Bronwyn waved her hand in a careless gesture. "Most crews on hijacked ships aren't hurt. Most are eventually released when the ransom's paid."

"Most," Morgan said, hanging on to her temper by a thread. "But that's not all, and not a cause to celebrate."

Bronwyn smiled, her long lashes dropping over her eyes, but not before Morgan caught the glittering animosity in the blue depths. "Was I celebrating? I hope not. That would be most insensitive of me, considering your father is being held hostage as we speak."

For a moment Morgan couldn't breathe. The air caught in her throat and she balled her hands into fists. "We'll have him home soon, though," she answered, struggling to sound calm. "Drakon's brought in the best to secure his release."

Bronwyn flashed Rowan an amused glance. "The best, yes, as well as the most expensive. What will the job cost Drakon this time, Rowan? Seven million? Ten? More?"

"That's none of your business, Bronwyn," Drakon said gruffly.

The Australian turned wide blue eyes on him. "You assigned me the task of improving the corporation's bottom line, which includes cutting unnecessary spending—"

"And you know perfectly well that I will pay Dunamas Maritime Intelligence from my personal account, not the corporation, so enough." Drakon's tone was cool and firm, but not cold or firm enough for Morgan.

Why did he put up with Bronwyn? Why did he allow his vice president to speak to him the way he did? He wouldn't tolerate it from anyone else, Morgan was sure of that.

"Yes, boss," Bronwyn answered, rolling her eyes even as she glanced in Morgan's direction, the exasperation in Bronwyn's eyes replaced by bruising disdain.

Interesting, Morgan thought, air catching in her throat. *Bronwyn doesn't like me, either.*

Morgan had sensed it five years ago, and had mentioned her concern to Drakon, but Drakon had brushed Morgan off, telling her not to be petty, that Bronwyn was far too professional to have any ill will toward his new wife. Morgan had felt ashamed for being petty—if that's what how she was behaving—and properly chastised, tried not to object to Bronwyn's frequent intrusions into their personal life, but it was almost impossible. Bronwyn called constantly, appeared on their doorstep at strange moments, felt perfectly comfortable drawing Drakon out of the living room and off into his study for long, private business conversations.

Morgan hated it, and had come to resent Bronwyn, all the while feeling guilty for resenting someone that Drakon viewed as so indispensible to his work.

But now Morgan knew she'd been right to object to Bronwyn's intrusiveness. Because Bronwyn meant to be intrusive. Bronwyn wanted Drakon. She'd wanted him five years ago, and she still wanted him now.

Of course, Morgan had no proof, just her female intuition and that nagging gut instinct that told her something was wrong...the same gut instinct that was telling her now that Bronwyn was still a problem.

Abruptly Morgan stood, unable to remain one more moment in the same room with Bronwyn.

"It's late and I'm still jet-lagged," Morgan said, her voice sharper than usual. "If you'll excuse me, I think I'll head to bed."

CHAPTER TEN

THE NEXT MORNING Morgan had coffee brought to her in her room and she sat on her balcony, sipping her coffee, trying to figure out how she could avoid going downstairs today. She'd slept like hell, dreaming of Bronwyn, as well as Bronwyn and Drakon frolicking in the pool, and the ballroom, and everywhere else, and the last person Morgan wanted to see was the real Bronwyn, who Morgan knew was up and about, as she could hear her voice wafting up from one of the terraces below.

Morgan glared down into her coffee as Bronwyn's laugh spiraled up again. Why was Bronwyn here? What was Drakon thinking?

"More coffee? A pastry?" a deep, distinctive male voice coming from the bedroom behind her, asked.

Morgan glanced over her shoulder, to where Drakon lounged in the doorway, looking horribly handsome and very rested. "You should knock," she said tartly, hating him for bringing Bronwyn here, to the villa, when Morgan was here feeling overwhelmed and out of control.

"I did. You didn't answer."

"Then maybe you shouldn't have come in."

"I needed to speak with you."

"But it's not polite to barge in on ladies in the morning."

"Not even if I have an invitation for an outing?"

That did give her pause, and Morgan eyed him suspiciously, excited at the idea of escaping the villa for a few hours, before realizing that she needed to be here, available, in case the pirates tried to contact her. "How can we just leave right now in the middle of everything? What if the pirates want to talk to me? Or change their demands?"

"They're not going to change their demands. They're anticipating six million dollars being delivered any day now."

He was probably right, and yet she found it hard to contemplate doing something pleasurable when her father was still in such trouble. "I wish I knew if he had his heart medicine. I wish I knew he was okay…healthy…strong. Then I'd feel better about things. But I don't know, and the not knowing is really scary."

"It's always the scariest part." His broad shoulders shifted. "But worrying doesn't change his situation, it just makes you sick, and makes it more difficult for you to cope with stress. Which is why I'm taking you out for a couple hours. Fresh air and a change of scenery will give you some perspective."

"And we could be reached if something happens?"

"Absolutely."

She hesitated. "So who would be going?"

"Just you and me, if that's all right."

Her gaze slowly swept over his face with the high cheekbones, straight nose, firm, sensual mouth, before dropping to his body. God, she loved his body…his narrow hips, his long lean, muscular torso and those sinfully broad shoulders. She glanced back up into his face, noting his arched eyebrow and his amused expression. She blushed. "Yes, that's all right."

His warm golden brown eyes, framed by those long, dense black lashes, glinted. "I'm glad."

She looked at him for a long moment, wondering what Drakon had up his sleeve, and why he'd decided to be charming today. He was reminding her of the Drakon of their courtship, the Drakon of their honeymoon—mellow, amusing, easygoing, attentive. She liked this Drakon, very much, but why was he here now? And what did he want? "When do we leave?"

"When can you be ready?"

They took the helicopter towards Naples, flying above the stunning Italian coastline, where the blue sea butted against the green swell of land, before rising up into the hills and the slopes of Mount Vesuvius, the volcano that had erupted and wiped out Pompeii.

"So beautiful," Morgan murmured, her fingers pressed against the slick helicopter window, her gaze fixed on the landscape below. "And so deceptively serene."

"Because Vesuvius is still active?"

"Isn't it considered one of the world's deadliest volcanoes?"

"Unfortunately, yes. Its Plinian eruptions aren't a good fit for the three million people living at the base, as well as up and down the slopes."

"I'd be afraid to live there."

"Scientists believe they can predict an eruption before it happens, and they do have an emergency evacuation plan.

She shivered. "I understand ancient Pompeii was beautiful."

"The villas that were on the outskirts of town would rival the finest villas today."

"I'd love to see it."

"Good. Because we're on our way there now."

Morgan clasped his arm in delight. "Really?"

"Really."

A bubble of warmth formed in her chest, rising. "I'm so glad!"

Drakon glanced down at her hand where it rested on his arm. He'd hardened the moment she touched him, it was how he always responded to her.

He drew a breath and exhaled, trying to ease some of

the tightness in his gut. "I hope you'll enjoy today," he said, grateful he could sound controlled even when he didn't feel that way. "I'm hoping you will find something in Pompeii to inspire you and your next jewelry collection."

"I don't think there will be another—"

"Yes, there will be."

"I made terrible mistakes—"

"Everyone makes mistakes, but that doesn't mean you should give up. You have a gift. You're an artist. I believe in your vision."

She looked up into his eyes, fear and hope in the blue depths. "Do you really mean that?"

"Absolutely. You will have more collections, and you will succeed."

"How can you be so certain?"

"Because I've seen what you can do, and I know you. You're truly talented, Morgan. There's no one else like you."

Drakon's car was parked at a helipad outside Pompeii, waiting for them, and the driver whisked them to the ancient city to meet a private guide who was going to take them on a behind-the-scenes tour of the ruined city.

Morgan was glad she'd worn flat leather sandals since they walked from one end of the city to another, and she listened closely to everything the guide said, captivated by his stories of first century Pompeii, a thriving city of approximately ten thousand people. She was fascinated by the buried city and its restaurants and hotels and brothels, as well as the artwork revealed…frescoes and mosaics and sculptures.

"Pompeii is the most incredible place," she said as they made their way through the extraordinary villa, House of the Faun, and back into the sunlight. "But Pompeii also breaks my heart. It was such a beautiful city, and so full of life and people and passion—and then it was all wiped out. Gone in a matter of hours."

"Are you sorry I brought you today?"

She shook her head. "No. It's amazing. All of it. The houses, the streets, the restaurants, the statues and pots and artifacts. But it hurts, too. Life is so fragile, and unpredictable. There are no guarantees. Not for anyone."

"Your life changed overnight, didn't it?"

She looked at him, suddenly wary. "You mean, with the revelation of Michael's Ponzi scheme?"

Drakon nodded and Morgan bit down into her lip. "It did," she agreed softly. "I still find it hard to believe what's happened at home. Who would have thought a year ago...even three months ago...that my father would become one of the most hated men in America? That we'd lose everything... that so many others would lose everything, too, through his, and Michael's, actions?"

They'd come to a stop next to the cordoned-off fountain with its bronze statue of a dancing faun. This beautiful solitary faun was all that was left of this once glorious, elegant garden, and she held her breath a moment, pressing a fist to her chest, as if somehow she could control the pain, ease the tenderness.

"My father was horrified when he discovered that all his clients, all his investors, had lost their money. He found out on his way to a Valentine's Day soiree—another one of those black-tie balls my mother loves—when he got the text from Michael to say that it was over. That agents from the federal government had just left his house and there would be arrests made, and that Dad should flee, rather than be indicted." Her voice faded and she struggled to continue. "At first Dad didn't believe it. None of us could believe it. And then when the shock wore off, there was anger, and shame."

Morgan worked her lip between her teeth, tasting blood but thinking nothing of it, because everything hurt now, all the time. Pain was constant. Pain and that endless, overwhelming shame. "Dad wanted to kill himself. My brother talked him out of it, telling Dad that if he was innocent, then he owed it to his family, his friends and his clients to prove his innocence, and try to recoup as much of the lost investments as he could. But then Dad vanished, and Mom said Dad would have been better off killing himself. That by disappearing, Dad had left us in a worse situation. Maybe Mom was right. Maybe Dad should have died—"

"You don't really feel that way," Drakon said brusquely. "Or you wouldn't be trying so hard to help him now."

"I guess part of me keeps hoping that if he returns, he can fix this...salvage something. Branson, you know, is determined to see all the investors paid back—"

"That's impossible."

"I know, but Branson can't escape his name. Women can marry and take a new surname. But Branson's a man. He'll be one of those hated Copelands forever."

"Someday people will forget. There will be other news that will become more urgent and compelling. There will be disasters and tragedies that will eventually cover this scandal, burying it."

Just as the volcano had buried Pompeii.

Morgan's gaze drifted slowly across the columns and walls and the sunken garden, feeling the emptiness, hearing the silence. Everything was so still here, and yet once this villa had bustled with life, with the comings and goings of the family and its household servants and pets. And all that activity and laughter and anger, all the fears and needs and dreams, ended that August day, and for hundreds of years this city lay buried beneath layers of ash and soil, grass and the development of new towns. New construction. New lives. New dreams.

"Come," Drakon said, putting his hand on her bare arm, his touch light, but steadying. "Let's walk. This place is making you sad, and I didn't bring you here to be sad. I brought you here to inspire you."

"I am inspired, and moved. Gives one perspective...and

certainly a great deal for me to be thankful for." She flashed Drakon an unsteady smile, allowing him to steer her from the garden and back to the street. "Like life. And air. And sunlight."

"Good girl. Count your blessings. Because you have many, you know. You have your health, and your creativity, and your brother and your sisters—"

"And you," she said, catching his hand, giving it a quick squeeze. "You've been here for me, and have hired Rowan to help rescue Dad. I am so grateful—"

"Please don't thank me."

"Then let me at least apologize, because I am sorry, Drakon, I am so, so sorry for what my father did, and deeply ashamed, too."

"You didn't do it, love. You aren't responsible."

"But he's my father."

"And maybe he didn't know that Amery was just depositing all that money into his own account. Maybe he had no idea. Perhaps you're right. Perhaps we wait to judge and try him, until he is back, and he can answer the charges, answer everyone's questions?"

Her heart surged, a little rush of hope, and she turned quickly to face him. "Do you really think he could be innocent? Do you think—" And then she abruptly broke off when she saw Drakon's face.

He didn't think her father was innocent. He still despised her father. Drakon was merely trying to soften the blow for her. Make her disillusionment and pain more bearable.

Her eyes burned and she looked away. "You don't have to do that," she whispered. "There's no need to say things you don't mean just to make me feel better. I'd rather hear the truth from you."

"And I'd rather protect you, *agapi mou.*"

Agapi mou. My love. Her chest squeezed, aching. "I remember when I really was your love."

"You will always be my love."

"But not the same way. It will never be the same."

"No, it won't be the same. It can't be."

He'd spoken gently, kindly, and for some reason that made it all even worse. "I hate what I did to us," she said. "Hate that I destroyed us."

"What did happen, Morgan? You were there one morning, and then gone that night. I just want to understand."

She hadn't planned on talking about what really happened, not here, not like this. "I wasn't prepared for life as a newly-wed," she said, stumbling a little over the words. "I...I had unrealistic expectations of our life in Greece."

"What did you think it would be like?"

"Our honeymoon."

"But you know I had to return to work."

"Yes, but I didn't know work for you meant twelve-hour days, every day." Her hands twisted anxiously. "And I understand now, that's just how you work, and I'm not criticizing you. But I didn't understand then, how it would be, and it didn't leave much time for me. I married you because I wanted to be with you, not because I wanted your money or a villa in Greece."

"Looking back, I know now I wasn't very flexible with my hours. I regret how much I worked."

"You loved your work."

"But I loved you more, Morgan."

She'd looked into his eyes as he said it and for a moment she was lost, his amber gaze that intense, searing heat of old, and her heart felt wrenched and she fought to hold back the tears.

She couldn't cry...couldn't cry...wouldn't cry....

"So where do we go now?" she murmured, holding back the tears by smiling hard, smiling to hide her pain and how much she'd missed Drakon, and how much she'd always love Drakon. "What's next on our tour?"

"Lunch," he said lightly, smiling back at her. "I've a restaurant in mind, it's on our way home in Sorrento."

They didn't actually eat in Sorrento, but at a restaurant just
outside the city, on the way to Positano. The simple one-
story restaurant was tucked high into the mountain, off the
beaten path, with a beamed ceiling and breathtaking views
of the coast.

Normally the restaurant just served dinner, but today
they'd opened for them for lunch, and Morgan and Drakon
had the place to themselves.

With the expansive windows open, and course after course
of the most delicious seafood and pasta arriving at their table,
Morgan felt the tension easing from between her shoulders.
After finishing her coffee, she leaned back in her chair. "This
was really lovely, Drakon. I feel almost optimistic again.
Thank you."

"I've done very little, Morgan."

"You've done everything. You've brought in Rowan and
his team, and while they work to free Dad, you're keeping
me occupied and encouraging me to think about life, down
the road. You've shown me incredible things today, and given
me ideas for future designs, and best of all, peace of mind.
You're my hero...my knight in shining armor."

"So much better than a husband."

"Husbands are overrated," she teased.

"Apparently so," he answered drily.

And then reality hit her, and the memory of what had happened to them. Her smile slowly, painfully faded. "I've cost
you a pretty penny, haven't I? Four hundred million here,
seven million there—"

"I don't think about the money when I look at you."

"What do you think about?"

"You."

She dipped her head, and while this is what she wanted

to hear, she did feel guilty. Love shouldn't be this expensive. Love shouldn't have cost Drakon so much. "I want to pay for Dunamas's services."

"They're expensive."

"But my father isn't your responsibility, and I can't allow you to keep picking up the tab, taking hits and losses, because you got tangled up with me."

"Tangled? Is that what they call wives and weddings these days?"

"Don't try to distract me. I'm serious about paying you back. It will take me some time. I'll pay in installments, but I'll pay interest, too. It's what the banks would do. And I may be one of those entitled Copelands, but I'm not entitled to your money, and I insist on making sure you are properly compensated—"

"You're ruining my lunch."

"You've finished eating, already."

"Then you're ruining my coffee."

"You've finished that, too." She held up a finger. "And before you think of anything else I'm ruining, please know I'm immensely grateful, which is why I'm trying to make things right, as well as make them fair."

"How is it fair for me to take what little money you earn over the next ten years? I'd be ashamed to take your money."

"And you don't think I'm ashamed that I had to come back to you, with my hand out, begging for assistance?"

Frowning, he pushed his empty cup. "We should go."

She reached across the table and caught his hand in hers. "Don't be angry, Drakon. Branson's not the only one who wants to put things right. If I could, I'd pay every one of my father's investors back—"

"You're not your father, Morgan. You're not responsible."

"I *feel* responsible."

"You'll make yourself sick, obsessing about this."

"And you don't obsess about what my father did to you?"

Drakon looked down at their hands, where their fingers were laced together. "Yes, I did lose a fortune," he said after a moment, his fingers tightening on hers. "But losing you five years ago was so much worse."

"No."

"Yes." He squeezed her fingers again. "There is always more money to be made, *gynaika mou.* But there is only one of you."

The driver stopped before the villa's great iron gates, waiting for them to open to give them access to the old estate's private drive and exquisite gardens. But Morgan wasn't ready to be back at the villa with Bronwyn and Rowan and the villa staff. After so many years of not being with Drakon, it was such a joy to have him to herself.

"We'll soon find out if Rowan's heard anything," Drakon said, glancing out the window as the four-story white marble villa came into view.

"Hopefully he has," she said, feeling guilty because for the past hour she hadn't thought of her father, not once. She'd been so happy just being with Drakon that she'd forgotten why she was here in Italy on the Amalfi Coast.

"And hopefully you had a good day," he added. "I'd thought perhaps you'd be inspired by Pompeii, but it can be overwhelming, too."

"I loved it. Every minute of it."

And it was true, she thought, as the car stopped in front of the villa's entrance and the driver stepped out to come around to open their door. But it wasn't just Pompeii she loved. She loved every minute of being with him today. This was what life was supposed to feel like. This is what she'd missed so much—his warmth, his strength, his friendship, his love.

His love.

She frowned, confused, suddenly caught between two worlds—the memories of a complicated past and the changing present. In this moment, the present, anything could happen. In this moment, everything was fluid and possible.

She and Drakon were possible. Life was possible. Love was possible.

She and Drakon could make different decisions, be different people, have a different future.

Could it be a future together?

"I enjoyed today, too," Drakon said.

"I hope we can do it again."

"Visit Pompeii?"

"Not necessarily Pompeii. But another outing...another adventure. It was fun."

Drakon suddenly leaned forward and swept the back of his hand over her cheek. "It was. And good to get away from here, and all this."

Her heart ached at the gentle touch. She'd forgotten how extraordinarily tender he could be. Over the years she'd focused on his control and his aloofness, in contrast to the wild heat of their lovemaking, and she'd turned him into someone he wasn't...someone cold and hard and unreachable. But that wasn't really Drakon. Yes, he could be aloof, and hard, and cold, but that wasn't often, and only when he was angry. And he wasn't always angry. In fact, he'd never been angry during their engagement or the first couple months of their marriage. It was only later, after they'd gone to Athens and gotten stuck in that terrible battle for control, a battle that had come to include Bronwyn, that they'd both become rigid and antagonistic.

She reached up, caught his hand, pressed it to her cheek. "Promise me we'll do this again soon. Please?"

"I promise," he said, holding her gaze as the driver opened the door to the back of the car.

Drakon stepped out and Morgan was just about to follow when heavy footsteps crunched the gravel drive and Rowan appeared at their side.

"Where have you been?" Rowan demanded. "I've been trying to reach you for the past hour."

"My mobile didn't ring," Drakon answered.

"I called," Rowan said. "Repeatedly." He turned to look at Morgan, his expression apologetic. "Your father was moved from his village today and we don't know where he is at the moment. But my office is gathering intelligence now that should help us understand what happened, why and where he's being held now."

CHAPTER ELEVEN

MORGAN PACED THE living room, unable to stop moving, unable to be still.

How could her father have vanished? Where had he been taken? And why? Had he gotten sick? Had he died? What were his captors reason for moving him?

She reached the end of the living room, turned and started back again. She'd traveled this path for ten minutes now but there was no way she could sit, not when fear bubbled up in her, consuming her.

Drakon was at the opposite end of the living room, watching her, keeping her company. "Where did they take him, Drakon?" she said, stopping midstep. "Why did they move him?"

She'd asked him the same questions already, several times, as a matter of fact, but he answered just as patiently now. "As Rowan explained, high-profile hostages are often moved from one location to another to stymie rescue attempts."

"Do you think they knew we were planning something?"

"I doubt it. Rowan doesn't think so, either, but we don't know for sure. Fortunately, his office is diligently gathering intelligence now and we should know more soon. Believe me, your father is at the top of Dunamas's priority list."

"He's right," Bronwyn said, entering the living room with a brisk step, her deceptively simple knit dress, the color of ripe plums, making the most of her lush shape. "Dunamas is pulling all their sources and resources from other tasks to gather information on your father, leaving dozens of ships, countless sailors and hundreds of millions of dollars of cargo vulnerable to attack."

"That's not necessary, Bron," Drakon said, rebuking her.

"But it's true." She leaned on the back of a wing chair, her blond hair smooth and sleek and falling forward in an elegant golden shimmer. The expression in her blue eyes was mocking and she shot Drakon a challenging glance. "I know you don't like to discuss business in front of your wife, but shouldn't she know the truth? That Dunamas is dropping everything, and everyone, because Morgan Copeland's criminal father has changed village locations?"

Morgan flinched at Bronwyn's words. "Is that true? Has Dunamas pulled all its surveillance and protection from its other clients?"

"No," Drakon said flatly. "It's not true. While Dunamas has made your father a priority, it continues its surveillance and protective services for each ship, and every customer, it's been hired to protect."

"But at tremendous personal expense," Bronwyn retorted.

"That's none of your business," he answered, giving her a look that would have crushed Morgan, but Bronwyn wasn't crushed.

"Funny how different you are when she's around." Bronwyn's blue gaze met his and held.

Drakon's jaw thickened. "I'm exactly the same."

"No. You're not. Normally Drakon Xanthis rules his shipping empire with a cool head, a critical eye and shrewd sense...always fiscally conservative, and cautious when it comes to expenses and investments." Bronwyn's lips pursed. "But the moment Morgan Copeland enters the picture, smart, insightful, strategic Drakon Xanthis loses his head. Suddenly money is no object, and common sense is thrown out the window—"

"Bronwyn," he growled.

The Australian jerked her chin up, her expression a curious mixture of anger and pain. "You're just a fool for love, aren't you?"

Drakon looked away, his jaw tight, his amber gaze strangely bleak. Morgan glanced from Drakon to Bronwyn and back again, feeling the tension humming in the room, but this wasn't the sparky, sexy kind of tension that zinged between her and Drakon, but something altogether different. This tension was dark and heavy and overwhelming....

It felt like death...loss...

Why? What had happened between them? And what bound Drakon to Bronwyn, a woman Morgan disliked so very intensely.

But then on her own accord, Bronwyn walked out, pausing in the doorway to look at Drakon. "Don't be putty in her hands," she said. "You know what happens to putty."

The pressure in Morgan's chest should have eased after Bronwyn left. There should have been a subtle shift in mood, an easing of the tension, some kind of relief.

But Morgan felt no relief, and from Drakon's taut features, she knew there would be no relief.

Whatever it was that Bronwyn had just said to Drakon—and Morgan had heard her, but hadn't understood the significance, only felt the biting sarcasm—it'd hit the mark. Drakon had paled and was now ashen, his strong jaw clenched so tightly the skin along the bone had gone white.

"What just happened?" Morgan asked, her voice cracking.

Drakon didn't answer. He didn't even look at her.

She flushed as silence stretched and it became evident that he wasn't going to answer her, either.

"What was she saying, Drakon?" Morgan whispered, hating the way shame crept through her, shame and fear and that terrible green-eyed monster called jealousy, because she was jealous of Bronwyn, jealous that Bronwyn could have such a powerful effect on Drakon.

But once again Morgan's question was met with stony silence. And the silence hurt. Not merely because he wasn't talking to her, but because Bronwyn had done this to him—to *them*—again.

Again.

Morgan's hands fisted at her sides. What was Bronwyn's power? Because she certainly had something...some strange and rather frightening influence over Drakon....

Something had to have happened between Drakon and Bronwyn. Something big...

Something private and powerful...

Morgan's head pounded as she left the living room. She needed space and quiet, and headed downstairs to the sunroom, and then outside to the broad terrace beyond. But the terrace still felt too confining and Morgan kept walking, down more stairs, to the lower garden, through manicured boxwood and fanciful hedges to the old rose garden and the herb garden and then to the miniature orchard with its peekaboo views of the sea.

She walked the narrow stone path through the orchard before reaching the twisting path that followed the cliff, the path dotted with marble benches. Morgan finally sat down in one of these cool marble benches facing the sea, and drew a slow breath, trying to process everything, from her father's disappearance, to Drakon and Bronwyn's peculiar relationship, to her own relationship with Drakon. There was a lot to sort through.

She sat on the bench, just breathing in the heady, fragrant scent of wisteria and the blossoms from the citrus trees in the small orchard, when she heard someone talking.

It was Rowan approaching on the path, talking on the phone, speaking English to someone, his tone clipped, no-nonsense, and his low brusque voice was such a contrast to his appearance. He looked like sex, but talked like a soldier. And suddenly the warrior king from the film *Spartacus* came to mind.

Rowan spotted her and ended his call.

"Any news about my father?" she asked him as he stopped before her bench.

"Not yet. But don't panic."

"I'm trying not to."

"Good girl."

The sun had dropped significantly and the colors in the sky were deepening, the light blue turning to rose gold.

"It's going to be another beautiful sunset," she said. "I love the sky here, the red and orange sunsets."

"You do know its pollution, ash and smoke just scattering away the shorter-wavelength part of the light spectrum."

Morgan made a face. "That's so not romantic."

He shrugged. "As Logan will tell you, I'm not a romantic guy."

Shocked, Morgan turned all the way to look at him. "You know my sister?"

"Drakon didn't tell you?"

"No."

"Thought he had."

"How do you know her?"

"I live in L.A. Malibu."

Which made sense as Logan lived in Los Angeles, too. "How well do you know her?"

He hesitated, just a fraction too long, and Morgan realized that he *knew* her, knew her, as in the Biblical knowing. "You guys...dated?"

"Not dated, plural. One date. Met at a celebrity fund-raiser."

"What fund-raiser?" she asked, finding it impossible to imagine Rowan Argyros at a charity event.

"It's inconsequential."

But from his tone, she knew it wasn't, and Morgan fought the sudden urge to smile. There was much more to the Rowan-Logan story than what he was telling her, and Morgan eyed him with new interest, as well as appreciation, because Logan might be her fraternal twin, but Logan and Morgan were polar opposites. Morgan was quieter and shyer, and Logan was extremely confident and extroverted, as well as assertive., especially when it came to men. Morgan had married Drakon, her first love, while Logan didn't believe in love.

"How did you two get along?" she asked now, lips still twitching, amused by the idea of Logan and Rowan together. They were both so strong—it would have been an interesting date...an explosive date.

"Fine."

"I doubt that."

Rowan looked at her from beneath a cocked brow, smiling, clearly amused. "Why do you say that?"

"Because I know Logan. She's my sister. And I've met you."

"Whatever happened—or didn't happen—is between your sister and me, but I will say she talked about you that night we were together. Told me...things...about you, and your past, not knowing I was connected to Drakon."

"Did you tell her you knew Drakon?"

"No."

"Well, there you go."

He stared down at her, expression troubled. He looked as if he wanted to say something but wasn't going to.

Morgan sighed. "What is it? What's on your mind?"

"Have you told Drakon about the year following your separation? Does he know what happened?"

Morgan eyed him warily. "About what?"

"About you being...ill."

She opened her mouth, and then closed it, shaking her head instead.

"Maybe you should. Maybe it's time."

Morgan turned back to the sea, where the horizon was now a dramatic parfait of pink and orange and red, with streaks of luscious violet. So beautiful it couldn't be real. "I don't think it'd change anything...if he knew."

"I think it would change a great deal. Maybe not for you, but for him."

She shot Rowan a cynical glance, feeling impossibly raw. "How so?"

"You weren't the only one who had a hard year after you left. Drakon's world fell apart, too."

Drakon was in his room, just stepping out of the shower when he heard a knock at his door. He dried off quickly, wrapped the towel around his hips and headed to the bedroom door. Opening it, he discovered Morgan in the hall.

"You okay?" she asked, looking up at him, a shadow of concern in her eyes.

He nodded. "I was just going to dress and come find you."

"Do you mind if I come in?"

He opened the door wider, and then once she was inside, he closed the door behind him.

"You look nice," she said, her voice low and husky.

"Almost naked?"

Color swept her cheeks. "I always liked you naked. You have an amazing body."

He folded his arms across his chest and stared at her. "I can't believe you came here to compliment my body."

"No...no. But it kind of...relates...to what I was going to say."

He rocked back on his hips, trying not to feel anything, even though he was already feeling too much of everything.

But wasn't that always the way it was when it came to Morgan? He felt so much. He loved her so much.

"Can I kiss you?" she blurted breathlessly.

He frowned, caught off guard.

"Just a kiss, for courage," she said, clasping her hands, nervously. "Because I don't know how to tell you this, and I'm not sure what you'll say, but I probably should tell you. 'Cause I don't think anyone did tell you—"

He drew her to him, then, silenced her stream of words with a kiss. His kiss was fierce, and she kissed him back with desperation, with the heat and hunger that had always been there between them.

He let the kiss go on, too, drawing her close to his body, cupping the back of her head with one hand while the other slid to the small of her back and urged her even closer to his hips. Just like that he was hard and hot and eager to be inside her body, wanting to fill her, needing to lose himself in her, needing to silence the voices in his head…voices of guilt and anger, failure and shame.…

But then Morgan ended the kiss and lifting her head she looked up into his eyes, her blue eyes wet, her black lashes matted. "I'm not right in the head." Her voice quavered. She tried to smile even as tears shimmered in her eyes. "I'm crazy."

"You're not crazy."

She nodded, and her lower lip quivered. "That's why you couldn't find me after I left you. I had a nervous breakdown. My family had me hospitalized."

Drakon flinched and stepped backward. "Why are you saying this?"

"It's what happened. I left you and I fell apart. I couldn't stop crying, and I couldn't eat, and I couldn't sleep, and everybody said it was this or that, but I just missed you. I wanted you."

"So why didn't you come back?"

"They wouldn't let me."

Drakon's gut churned, and his hands clenched involuntarily at his side. "*Who* wouldn't let you?"

"The doctors. The hospital. My family. They made me stay there at McLean. It's a...mental...hospital."

"I know what McLean is." Drakon looked at her in barely masked horror. "I don't understand, Morgan. You were there...why?"

"Because I was crazy."

"You *weren't* crazy!"

"They said I was." She walked away from him, moving around his room, which had been their room on their honeymoon. She touched an end table, and the foot of the bed, and then the chaise in the corner before she turned to look at him. "And I did feel crazy...but I kept thinking if I could just get to you, I'd feel better."

"So why didn't you come home to me?"

"I couldn't." She struggled to smile, but failed. "I couldn't get to you, couldn't call you or write to you. They wouldn't let me do anything until I calmed down and did all the therapy and the counseling sessions—"

"What do you mean, they wouldn't let you out? Didn't you check yourself in?"

She shook her head, and sat down on the chaise, smoothing her skirt over her knees. "No. My parents did. My mother did. My dad approved, but it was Mother who insisted. She said you would never want me back the way I was." Morgan looked up at him, eyes bright, above the pallor of her cheeks. "So I went through the treatment, but it didn't help. It didn't work. They wanted me to say I could live without you, and I couldn't."

"Why not?"

Her slim shoulders lifted and fell. "Because I couldn't."

"So why did you leave me in the first place?"

"I started falling apart in Ekali. I was fine when we first

got there, but after the first month, something happened to me. I began to cry when you were at work and I tried to hide it from you when you came home, but you must have known, because you changed, too. You became colder and distant, and maybe it wasn't you...maybe it was all me... because I needed too much from you, and God knows, my needs weren't healthy—"

"And who told you that you needs weren't healthy?" he growled, trying desperately hard to hang on to his temper. "Your parents?"

"And the doctors. And the therapists."

"Christ," he muttered under his breath, dragging a hand through his hair. "That's not true, you know," he said, looking at her. "You were young and isolated and lonely and I wasn't there for you. I know that now. I know I wasn't fair to you. I worked ridiculous hours, and expected you to be able to entertain yourself, and I owe you an apology. Actually, I owe you many, many apologies."

She managed a small, tight smile. "It's hard to remember... hard to go back...because what we had was good, so good, and then it all became so bad...." She sighed and rubbed her head. "I wish we could go back, and do it all again, and make different decisions this time."

"There's no going back, though, only going forward."

Morgan nodded. "I know, and I'm trying. And seeing Pompeii with you today made me realize that we have to go forward. We have to have hope and courage and build new lives."

He came to her, crouched before her, his hands on either side of her knees, his gaze searching hers. "I know I failed you—"

"No more than I failed you, Drakon."

"But you didn't fail me. You were perfect...you were warm and real and hopeful and sensitive."

"So why did you pull away? Why shut me out...because it felt like you did—"

"I did. I definitely shut you out, and you weren't imagining that I pulled away, because I did that, too."

"Why?"

He hesitated a moment and then drew a breath. "Because I loved you so much, and yet I was overwhelmed by feelings of inadequacy...I couldn't make you happy, I couldn't meet your needs, I couldn't be who or what you wanted, so I...pushed you away."

Her eyes searched his. "It wasn't my imagination?"

"No."

"I wasn't crazy when I left you then?"

"No."

She made a soft, hoarse sound. "So I just went crazy when I left you."

"You were never crazy, Morgan."

She smiled, sadly. "But I was. Leaving you tore me apart. I felt my heart break when I left you. Everyone kept telling me I was developing this disorder or that disorder but they didn't understand...I just needed you. I just wanted you. And they wouldn't let me have you." Tears filled her eyes. "No one believed that I could love you that deeply...but why was it wrong to love you so much? Why did it make me bad... and mad...to miss you that much?"

"They were wrong, Morgan. And I was wrong. And I know you weren't insane, because I felt the same way, too. And I couldn't get to you, either. I couldn't find you, and all I wanted was to find you and apologize, and fix things, and change things, so that we could be happy. I knew we could be happy. I just needed you home."

She reached up to knock away a tear before it could fall. "But I didn't come back."

"No. But I wouldn't give up on you, or us. I still can't give up on us." He reached out to wipe her cheek dry with his thumb. "Tell me, my love, that I haven't waited in vain. Tell me there's a place in your life for me. Give me hope, Morgan."

She just looked at him, deep into his eyes, for a long moment before leaning forward and kissing him. "Yes," she whispered against his mouth. "Yes, there's a place in my life for you. There will always be a place in my life for you. I need you, Drakon. Can't live without you, Drakon."

His mouth covered hers, and he kissed her deeply, but it wasn't enough for her. Morgan needed more, craved more, and she wrapped her arms around his neck, and opened her knees so he could move between them, his big body pressed against hers. Still kissing her, he pressed her back onto the chaise, his towel falling off as he stretched out over her, his hand sliding up her rib cage to cup her breast.

Morgan hissed a breath as his fingers rubbed her nipple, making the sensitive peak pucker and tighten. His other hand was moving down her torso, tugging up the hem of her dress, finding her bare inner thigh, his touch sending lightning forks of sensation zinging through her body, making her body heat and her core melt. She wanted him, wanted him so much, and she sucked on his tongue, desperate for him to strip her and feel his warm, bare skin on hers.

And then his phone rang on the bedside table, chiming with a unique ringtone that Morgan had never heard before.

He lifted his head, listened, frowning. "Damn."

"What?"

He shook his head and rolled away from her, leaving the chaise to pick up his phone from the table near the bed. "Damn," he muttered, reading the message. "She needs to talk to me before she returns to Athens."

Morgan didn't even need to ask who "she" was, knowing perfectly well it was Bronwyn. "Now?"

"She's leaving soon. Tonight."

"Surely she can wait a half hour?"

He didn't answer immediately, simply rolled away, his towel falling off in the process. "I won't be long."

"You really have to go now?"

"I'll be back in less than fifteen minutes."

Morgan watched him walk, without a stitch of clothing, to the closet. Dressed, Drakon Xanthis was a handsome, sophisticated man. Naked, he was absolutely beautiful.

He was beautiful now, and her mouth dried, her heart hurting as he disappeared into the closet, his body tan, skin gleaming, his muscles taut. Honed. He had those big shoulders and broad chest and lean flat abs and long strong legs, and between those legs hung his thick shaft, impressive even now, when he wasn't erect.

As the closet light came on, Morgan felt a surge of jealousy, hating that Drakon and his beautiful, hard, honed body was leaving her to go meet Bronwyn.

When he emerged a few minutes later, buckling the belt on his trousers, buttoning his shirt and tucking it into the waistband, Morgan felt almost sick.

Suddenly she felt like the young bride she'd been five years ago...uncertain, insecure, overwhelmed by her new life as Drakon Xanthis's American bride.

Drakon must have seen her fear because his brow furrowed as he gazed down at her. "There's no need to be threatened by Bronwyn. She works for me, but you're my wife."

But she'd been his wife before, and it hadn't helped her feel secure, or close to him. And while she'd been home alone for twelve, fourteen, sometimes sixteen hours a day, he'd been at the office with Bronwyn. Even if there was nothing sexual between him and Bronwyn, by virtue of being his trusted right hand, Bronwyn still got to spend time with Drakon...time Morgan would love to have. Not because Morgan couldn't be alone and needed Drakon to prop her up, but because she loved Drakon and enjoyed his company more than anyone else.

"I just don't want to feel as if I have to fight Bronwyn for you anymore," she said quietly, calmly, grateful that her voice could sound so steady when her heart was racing so fast.

"But you don't have to fight Bron for me. You never have."

And while this conversation was brutal, it was also necessary and long overdue. They should have talked about Bronwyn years ago. Morgan should have told Drakon how uncomfortable she was around her when they first married, but she hadn't, too afraid of displeasing him. And so the wound had festered, and her fear grew, until their entire relationship had become stunted and toxic.

"You love me?" she whispered.

"How can you doubt it?"

She bit down into her lip, holding back her fears, and her need to be reassured, knowing that her fears were irrational. Drakon wouldn't be here, helping her, if he didn't want to be. Drakon wouldn't have brought in Rowan to rescue her father if he didn't care about her. It was time she stopped panicking and stopped allowing her insecurities to get the upper hand. Drakon loved her. Drakon had always loved her. But he wasn't a woman...he was a man, a Greek man that had been raised to conceal vulnerabilities and avoid emotion. "I don't doubt it," she whispered. "I know you love me. Without question."

"There is no competition between you and Bron," he said roughly, his handsome, chiseled features hard.

She nodded, wanting to believe it, needing to believe it, but as he'd told her once, actions spoke louder than words. If he stayed at his office night after night until ten, making decisions, talking with Bronwyn, how was Morgan supposed to feel?

She felt a twinge of panic at the idea of returning to that life, but she had to be strong and confident. She believed in Drakon, and she had to believe that Drakon would do what was right for her...for them.

"Promise me you're not threatened by her," he said, stalking closer to her, forcing her to tilt her head back to meet his eyes.

"Promise me you won't be upset if I have to work long days, and late into the night, with her," he added.

Morgan's mouth opened, closed. She wanted to tell him she'd be fine, and she would try to be fine with it, but she couldn't promise him she'd be perfectly comfortable. She didn't know any woman who'd be perfectly comfortable with her husband being alone with a gorgeous woman night after night…day after day. Working in such close proximity created an intimacy that could lead to other things…and Morgan was sure Bronwyn did have feelings for Drakon. In fact, Morgan was sure Bronwyn was the problem here, not Drakon, but how could she tell him that?

She couldn't. But she also couldn't lie. And so with her heart racing, she swallowed convulsively. "I'm here for the long haul, Drakon. I'm here to stay. I'm playing for keeps."

His amber gaze drilled into her. "Playing for keeps," he repeated softly.

She licked her dry lips. "Yes."

"Is that a threat or a promise?"

"It's whatever you want it to be."

He laughed once, the mocking sound such a contrast to the sudden fire in his eyes. And then he was gone, walking out, leaving the door wide open behind him.

CHAPTER TWELVE

HE WASN'T GONE just a few minutes. He was gone a long time, over an hour, and Morgan returned to her room, wondering if she should dress for dinner, or if dinner would even be served tonight as it was growing late, well past the time they normally gathered in the living room for *aperitivos*.

Morgan eventually did change and go downstairs. Rowan was in the living room, having a drink.

"Can I pour you something?" he offered as she entered the candle lit living room.

"The Campari," she said, even as she tried to listen to the house, trying to hear where Drakon and Bronwyn might be.

Rowan filled her glass, handed her the cocktail. "They're outside," he said. "Or they were."

She sipped the cocktail. Campari and orange. It was tart and sweet at the same time. "Why do you say, 'were'?"

"A car arrived a half hour ago, and it just pulled away a few minutes ago." Rowan turned, nodded at the hall. "And here he is. Drakon Xanthis in the flesh." Rowan raised his glass. "I've a few calls to make. I'll have more privacy elsewhere. Cheers." And then Rowan walked out, leaving Drakon and Morgan alone.

Drakon walked past Morgan without saying a word, going to the bar where he made himself a drink. Morgan watched him, wondering what had happened between him and Bronwyn.

Drakon carried his drink to the window, where he sipped it and stared out at the dark sky.

"She's gone," he said at last. "Back to Athens."

Morgan looked at his rigid back, and the set of his shoulders. "Did something happen?" she asked quietly.

"I let her go."

"What?"

"I let her go. Fired her. Terminated her employment. Whatever you want to call it."

"Why?"

"I watched her here, how she behaved around you, and I didn't like it. She has worked for me for a long time—eight years—and she was good at what she did, but I won't have any woman snubbing you, not anymore. I won't look the other way, especially if it's my employee, or a friend of mine. It's not acceptable, and you shouldn't have to endure slights and snubs...not from anyone."

Morgan heard what he was saying and appreciated everything he was saying, but there was something else happening here. Drakon was upset...angry...but Morgan didn't understand who he was upset with—Bronwyn, himself, or Morgan.

"You didn't have to fire her because of me," Morgan said, choosing her words carefully. "I meant it when I said, I was sticking around. I'm not going to let anyone scare me away. I'm not twenty-two anymore. I'm twenty-seven and I know a lot more about the world now, and a lot more about myself."

He sipped his cocktail. "I agree you've changed, but I've also changed, and Bronwyn has, too. There was a time I needed her—and she saved me, I owe her a lot, if not everything—but that was four years ago, and things are different and it's time for her to move on. It'll be better for her."

Morgan's inside flipped nervously. "How did she save you?"

He took another long drink from his crystal tumbler and then looked over his shoulder at Morgan. "If it weren't for her, I wouldn't have a company. I wouldn't have this villa. I wouldn't have anything."

"I don't understand."

"I know you don't." He sighed, shrugged, took another quick drink before continuing. "I would prefer you didn't know, and I'd promised Bron years ago I wouldn't tell you, she didn't want me to tell you. She said you wouldn't like it… you wouldn't respect me…but that's a risk I'll have to take."

Morgan sat down in one of the chairs. "Please tell me."

He walked the length of the room, and it was a long room, before dropping into a chair not far from hers. "A number of years ago, I made a mistake. Normally it wouldn't be an issue, but with the situation being what it was, the mistake was serious. It nearly bankrupted me."

He closed his eyes, shook his head, then opened them again and looked at her. "I was close to losing everything. And I mean everything. The company. The ships. The contracts. Our offices. Our homes. The cars, planes, yachts… everything…" His voice faded and for a moment there was just silence, a heavy, suffocating silence that blanketed the room. "And the worst of it was, I didn't care."

Drakon was still looking at her, but he didn't seem to see her. He seemed to be seeing something else, his expression tortured. "I didn't care," he repeated lowly, strangely detached.

Morgan had never heard him talk this way, or sound this way, and her heart thumped uncomfortably and she wasn't sure if she wanted to hear more, but there was no way she would stop him from talking.

After a long, uneasy moment Drakon continued. "I wasn't able to make good decisions during this time, and I didn't do what I should have done to protect my company, my future, or my employees. I was willing to lose it all. But Bronwyn refused to just stand there, a witness, as my company and life imploded."

"So she took over," he continued. "She stepped into my empty shoes and vacant office and became me...became president and CEO and no one knew it was Bronwyn Harper forging my signature, shifting funds, slashing spending, liquidating assets." Drakon's gaze met Morgan's. "Not all of her decisions were the right ones. Some of her actions had negative consequences, but if she hadn't stepped in when she did, there would be nothing here today."

It was hard for Morgan to hear Drakon speak of Bronwyn so reverently, because Morgan wished she'd been the one who had been there for Drakon when he needed someone. "I'm glad she helped you," Morgan said huskily. "Glad she was able to help you, because I couldn't have, even if I'd wanted to."

He looked at her, amber gaze piercing. "So yes, she helped me, but she was never more than a valuable employee. She was never your rival. I never once wanted her. I have only wanted you."

"Then why fire her? If she was such a help, and you feel so grateful—"

"She wanted more than what we had." His mouth curved but the smile didn't reach his eyes. "She made it clear she wanted more, that she was in love with me, but I didn't feel that way about her. I loved you, and only you, and Bronwyn knew that."

"But she stuck around all these years...she stuck around because she had to hope she had a chance."

He shrugged. "Maybe. Probably. But she didn't. If I couldn't have you, there wouldn't have been anyone else for me. It was you or nobody."

Morgan exhaled slowly, her head spinning. "She must be heartbroken right now."

"She'll be fine. She's strong. She's smart. She'll have a better life now, away from me." Drakon drew Morgan into his arms and pressed a kiss to her temple, and then another to her cheekbone. "It's you I'm worried about."

"You don't need to worry about me."

"Rowan hasn't found your father yet."

"But he hasn't given up."

"No. And Rowan won't, not until we find your father. There is no one better than Rowan and Dunamas. They will continue looking for your father, until he is found."

"What if it takes weeks...months...years?"

"Doesn't matter. I promise you, we will never forget him, and never give up."

CHAPTER THIRTEEN

THEY ATE DINNER, just the two of them, as Rowan was nowhere to be found, and then skipping coffee and dessert, they headed upstairs to Drakon's room, where they made love, soundlessly, wordlessly, so quiet in the dark silent night.

Their lovemaking wasn't fierce and hot, or carnal and raw, but slow, careful, tender, so tender that Morgan wept after she climaxed because she'd never felt this way with Drakon before, had never made love with him like this before, their bodies so close, so connected, they'd felt like one.

Afterward, they lay side by side, his body wrapped around hers, his muscular arm holding her close to him, and still they said nothing, because there were no words, at least not the right ones. So much had happened since they'd met. So much love and yet so much loss. So much anger and pain and heartbreak...

But words right now wouldn't help, words would just get in the way, so they didn't talk, but instead lay close, filled with emotion, intense emotion that surged and ached and trembled and twisted.

Lying there in the dark, wrapped in Drakon's warmth and listening to him breathe, Morgan knew these things—she still loved him, deeply, passionately.

She also knew she wouldn't leave him. Not ever again.

But for them to have a future, they would have to talk

more, and they'd need patience, forgiveness, courage and strength.

She knew she was willing to fight for Drakon and her marriage, but there were still things she didn't understand about Drakon, things she didn't understand about the past.

And when, a half hour later, he kissed her shoulder but eased away to climb from the bed, she was filled with unease.

Turning over, she watched as he stepped into his cotton pajama pants, settling the drawstring waist low on his hips, leaving that magnificent torso bare. She watched him walk to the French door and push open the curtains. Propping an arm against the glass, he stared out at the sea, which rippled silver with moonlight.

She sat up and wrapped an arm around her knees, pressing the covers closer to her legs. "I've been thinking about what you said earlier, and how you feel so grateful to Bronwyn for saving your company...and saving you...when you made a mistake and nearly lost everything. But I know you. You don't make mistakes. What mistake did you make, that could have possibly cost you your company?"

He said nothing right away and Morgan was afraid he wouldn't speak, but then he shrugged. "I was distracted. Wasn't focused on work. And suddenly there was no money. No money to pay anybody, no money for taxes, no money at all."

"How could there be no money? Where did it go?"

Again, another long, excruciating silence. "Bad investments."

Ice filled her veins and she flashed to her father, and Michael Amery. No...he wouldn't...not a second time. She held her breath, even as her heart began to race. "You said...bad investments....plural." Morgan swallowed around the lump of panic forming in her throat. "Did you mean, investments, plural, or was there just that one horrible, huge loss to my father?"

He was silent so long that bile rose up in her throat, and she knew, she knew, there was more. She knew something else had happened, something he'd never told her. "Drakon, *agapo mou,* please, please tell me."

Drakon shifted his weight, muscles ripping across his shoulders and down his back, and then he turned toward her, the moonlight glancing briefly over his features until he'd turned his back to the window, with the light behind him, shadowing his face again. "Your father came to me asking for help after you'd left me."

Pain shot through her. Tears filled her eyes. "You gave him more money."

Drakon's lips compressed. "He was your father. He needed help."

"How much did he ask for?"

"A billion."

"Oh, my God." She pressed her hand to her mouth. "Drakon, no. You didn't..."

"What was I to do, Morgan? He was in trouble. I was his son-in-law, and I loved you. Family is family—"

"But I'd left you!"

"But I hadn't left you."

She ground her teeth together, tears blinding her, her stomach churning in bitter protest. "I can't believe this."

He laughed hollowly. "When your father came to me, telling me he was in trouble...that he had investors who needed their money back, but he didn't have the liquidity to give them their money...I thought it was my chance to win you back. But I didn't have that kind of money sitting in an account, no one has money like that, so I took loans from banks, as well as other resources, to come up with the money for your father."

"And you didn't get me back, did you?" she whispered.

For a minute there was just silence, and an almost unbearable pain, and then Drakon shook his head. "No. I gave him the money but Daniel refused to tell me where you were. Said that you'd contact me when you were ready."

"And I couldn't contact you, not at McLean." She blinked to clear her eyes. "And then what happened?"

"The economy started crashing. My creditors and lenders began to call their loans. But there was no money to give them. There was nothing I could do but file for bankruptcy, and fold. And I was fine with that, because without you, I didn't care."

"You're breaking my heart," Morgan whispered.

"I was pathetic. Bron said you'd find me pathetic—"

"Pathetic? How could I find you, who sacrificed everything for me, pathetic?" She rose up on her knees. "You were a hero. You loved me. You fought for me. You were willing to sacrifice everything for me."

He turned and looked at her, his face still shadowed but she felt his intensity. "I don't want to live without you, Morgan. I don't like life without you. And maybe that's weak—"

"Not weak," she said, leaving the bed to go to him, wrap her arms around his waist. She held him tightly, chilled by what he had told her, as well as chilled by the reality of her parents taking her to McLean and leaving her there when they knew Drakon wanted her, when they knew Drakon loved her. She didn't understand their motivations, but then, their lives were about money and appearances and Morgan knew she'd embarrassed them by coming home from Greece, heartbroken and hysterical.

He slid a hand down her back, shaping her to him. "I don't think you understand how much I loved you," he said roughly. "How much I will always love you." His voice cracked, turned hoarse. "There is no one else for me, but you. You aren't just my wife. You are my world."

"And you are mine."

"Why did you leave then?"

"I was honestly falling apart."

"Why?"

"I loved you so much, it scared me. I'd never felt for anyone what I felt for you…but the feelings were so intense, it made me feel out of control. And then when we made love… that started to do something to my head. Played games with me, made me afraid."

"Afraid? Why? How?"

"I had so little experience when I met you, and you had so much, and in bed you're…hot. Erotic. Demanding. You make everything hot and erotic, too."

"I demanded too much of you?"

"There were times I felt overwhelmed."

"Thus, your disgust."

"You never disgusted me. I shouldn't have said that. It wasn't true. I was just angry and hurt, and trying desperately hard to keep you at arm's length since I find you impossible to resist."

He stepped away from her and went to flip the light switch, turning on the small wall sconces so the room glowed with soft yellow light. "Maybe I didn't disgust you, but I must have scared you at times for you to even say such a thing."

"I never minded it being…hot…when you were relaxed with me, and spent a lot of time with me, but once we returned to Athens, I didn't see you often and then we weren't talking and it didn't feel the same. It didn't feel as warm and safe. It felt more dangerous."

"But you always came."

"Because you've got great technique." She managed an unsteady smile. "But I'd rather not come, and just be close to you, feel close to you, than have erotic sex and have you feel like a stranger."

He sat down on the side of the bed. "Come here." He smiled crookedly. "Please."

Morgan walked to him, heart thumping, and feeling painfully shy. "Yes?"

He drew her down onto the bed next to him, and kissed her, once and again, before lifting his head to look down into her eyes. "I love how sensual you are. I love your passionate nature. But I never want you to be uncomfortable with me again...in bed, or out of bed. I love you too much to hurt you or scare you or to push you away. But you have to tell me when something is too much. You have to tell me when I'm being distant or when you feel nervous or lonely or afraid."

"You want me to talk to you," she said.

"Yes. I want you to talk to me."

"That means you have to talk to me, too."

He smiled even more crookedly. "I know."

"Okay."

"But I don't want you bored...especially in bed."

"My God, Morgan, I could never be bored in bed with you."

"No?"

"No! When we're together it's not about sex...its about me showing you how much you mean to me. How much I cherish you. How much I worship you. When I touch you, Morgan, I'm telling you that nothing is more important to me than you, and that I love you with all of my heart, and all of my soul."

"Really?"

"Really." His gaze searched hers. "All I have wanted for these past five years is to have you come home. I want you home. Morgan, please come home with me—"

"Yes." She reached up, cupped his cheek, drawing his face toward hers. She kissed him, deeply, and a shiver raced through her as his tongue met hers, teasing her. "Yes. I'm staying with you, going home with you, back to Athens."

"Even though you hate that white ice cube tray?" he asked, turning his mouth into her hand and kissing her palm.

Another delicious shiver ran through her and she smiled.

"But would you mind if I added a few colorful rugs? A few paintings…some throw pillows?"

"Maybe what we really need is a new house for a fresh start—"

"No."

"Yes. I don't like the house, either."

"What?"

He laughed softly. "I hate it. It's awful. I never liked it. Not while they were building it, and not even when we moved in, but I thought you did like it, so I never told you."

"I think we have a slight communication problem," she said drily.

"You think?" he teased, pressing her backward onto the bed, and then stretching out over her, his long hard body covering hers.

"We need to work on it."

"Mmm," he agreed, kissing her throat and pushing the covers down to bare her breasts. "We're going to have to start talking more," he said, alternately kissing and licking the slope of her breast.

She sighed and arched as he latched onto one of her tight, pebbled nipples. "Okay," she gasped, desire coiling in her belly.

"Do you like this?" he asked, as he stroked down her flat belly.

"Um, yes."

"And this?" he asked, his fingers slipping between her legs.

She gasped as he caressed her most sensitive spot. "Yes. And I'm glad we're talking…but do we have to do it now?"

She felt his silent laughter as his teeth scraped her nipple. "No," he answered. "I'd much rather just concentrate on you, and making you come."

"Good."

She gasped again as his fingers slipped down, where she

was slick and wet, and then caressed up over the nub again. "Drakon?"

"Yes, *gynaika mou?*"

"Make love to me. And love me. Forever."

He shifted, bracing his weight on his arms and looked down into her eyes for an endless moment. "Always. Always, and forever, until I die."

EPILOGUE

"WILL YOU DO it, Logan? Cover for me for a few days so Drakon and I can have a brief getaway?" Morgan asked, speaking
calmly into the phone, trying to sound relaxed, even though
she was frustrated with Logan for dodging her calls for the
past week. "You'd just be a point person for a few days, if
there are any communication issues, but I doubt there will be."

"I can't drop everything and take over Dad's search just so
you and Drakon can have a second honeymoon," Logan said,
her voice sharp on the speakerphone. "Some of us have jobs,
Morgan. Some of us must work as we don't have wealthy
husbands to take care of us."

"Would you like a wealthy husband, Logan?" Drakon said,
unable to remain silent in his seat across from Morgan's on
his private jet. They were still on the ground, hadn't closed
the doors, because Morgan had refused to take off until
Logan promised she'd help. "You know it can be arranged."

"No, thank you, Drakon. I am quite capable of taking care
of myself," Logan retorted crisply.

Drakon smiled. "You might actually enjoy a strong Greek
husband…almost as much as he'd enjoy managing you."

"Not going to happen," Logan snapped. "But if it will help
me get off this call, then yes, Morgan, I will be your contact
person should something happen while you and Drakon are
doing whatever you and Drakon do."

Drakon arched a brow at Morgan, and Morgan shook her

head at him, blushing. "I seriously doubt anything will happen, though. We're only going to be gone a few days...just for a long weekend—"

"I got it. You're just gone a few days. Dunamas is doing all the intelligence work and orchestrating the rescue. They'll call me if they can't reach you should there be developments." Logan paused. "Did I forget anything?"

Morgan grimaced. "No. That's pretty much it."

"Good. Now go...scram. Enjoy your trip. And try to have fun. Dad's going to be okay." Logan's voice suddenly softened. "I'll make sure he is, I promise."

Morgan hung up and looked at Drakon, who had just signaled to his flight crew that they were ready to take off. "Why am I worrying so much?"

His amber gaze met hers. "Because you deliberately withheld information from her, knowing she'd never agree to help us if she thought she'd have to deal with Rowan."

Morgan chewed on her lip. "Let's just hope she doesn't have to deal with him. Otherwise there's going to be hell to pay."

"Rowan said the exact same thing."

* * * * *